HAPPILY EVER
Ashten

- a novel –

Erynn

Mangum

Erynn Mangum

Cover design by Paper and Sage Designs

Unless otherwise noted, scripture taken from the NEW
AMERICAN STANDARD BIBLE®, Copyright © 1960, 1962, 1963,
1968, 1971, 1972, 1973, 1975, 1977, 1995 by The Lockman
Foundation. Used by permission.

OTHER NOVELS
BY ERYNN MANGUM

THE LAUREN HOLBROOK SERIES
Miss Match

Rematch

Match Point

Match Made

Bake Me A Match

THE MAYA DAVIS SERIES
Cool Beans

Latte Daze

Double Shot

THE PAIGE ALDER SERIES
Paige Torn

Paige Rewritten

Paige Turned

Erynn Mangum

This book is dedicated to three small people,
without whom it would have been written a lot sooner
but not had nearly as much depth:
Nathan, Parker and Eisley
You are all my favorite. I love you very much!

Eryun Mangum

CHAPTER *One*

I remember reading books when I was about fifteen and the protagonists would be thirty-one years old and I would think to myself, "I wonder why the author chose to make that character so old?"

Now, I look in the mirror and make a face at the wrinkles I can see forming by my eyes. Thirty-one today.

I don't feel old.

This mirror is begging to differ. Despite the good three ounces of concealer that I have mashed into my under-the-eye circles.

Time to leave the bathroom. I walk back across the dark hall into my little room that I rent from my friend, Katie McCoy.

The summer, for most of my fellow teacher friends, is all about relaxing. Most of them do absolutely nothing all summer or go on these awesome vacations with their families or catch all the new movies in the theaters or whatever they feel like doing at the time.

I, though, am a Wadeley. And goodness only knows that Wadeleys rarely relax. Even on days off, my parents don't sit still.

Once, when I was about fifteen and I was too young to know better, I tried to use the Genesis tactic on my parents. You know, God made the world in six days and then relaxed on the seventh and maybe we might want to try that out one day?

Bless my heart. So young, so dumb.

I pull on my work clothes and tie my ugly, non-skid work shoes.

The plan for today is to get through it without every person I know making a big deal about it being my birthday.

I sneak down the hallway, trying to stay as quiet as possible, though I've definitely dropped a pan on accident one morning and Katie didn't wake up. Still, I don't even breathe as I tiptoe down the dark hallway.

"Happy birthday!"

I scream and crash straight into the wall.

Katie is laughing so hard she's doubled over and her long blonde hair is dangerously close to the blueberry muffin she's holding with a lit candle sticking out of it.

I shake my head and take the muffin from her. "Thanks."

"You scare easily."

"You aren't supposed to be up baking." I frown at her. "When did you get up?"

"I baked those yesterday. I got up about three minutes ago. And I'm going back to bed now."

Considering Katie's normal wake up time, I'm super touched. "Thanks, friend."

"You're welcome. Happy birthday, old woman."

I sigh. "Thanks, friend." This time, there's some sarcasm in my tone.

"Welcome to the club." She grins at me, tugging her robe closer around her.

I'm fairly certain that despite our identical age, I am not anywhere close to being in the same club as Katie. She's seriously one of the most naturally beautiful people I've ever met. And I see her without makeup frequently.

If Luke doesn't propose here soon, he's officially lost his mind.

Luke Brantley is Katie's boyfriend and they've been dating pretty seriously for a little while now. He's a nice guy. He's a little too nice, honestly. I've never seen the man upset about anything.

He's like Mr. Rogers in a thirty-something-year-old body.

It's disconcerting. You should have more than one emotion.

He even wears cardigans.

9

I mean, to each their own. Maybe Katie prefers her men to have one default mode. Predictable, easy to understand.

Just weird, if you ask me.

But I come from the Missouri equivalent of *My Big Fat Greek Wedding*, so maybe I'm the one who is weird.

Except when it comes to cardigans.

I'm sorry. Men should not wear cardigans.

"Well, are you going to blow out the candle?" Katie asks me, nodding to the still-lit muffin in my hand. "Notice that I was kind and didn't try to fit all thirty-one candles on the one muffin."

"Thanks."

"No problem. Make a wish."

My family had this thing that you aren't really the age you are turning on your birthday until you blow out the birthday candles.

Here we go, Thirty-One.

I take a deep breath, blow lightly and the candle is instantly extinguished.

"Nice. What did you wish for?"

"You can't tell people or it doesn't come true."

"You didn't wish for anything, did you?" Katie asks me.

"Bye Katie. Thanks for the muffin."

"Good night, Ashten. Enjoy your day." Katie grins and walks back down the hall. I take my muffin and go out the front door, locking it as I leave.

Sometimes I'm super envious of Katie and her mostly work-from-home job.

Minnie's Diner is right on the outskirts of town and we have enough parking here to fit about eighty of those giant tour buses that grandparents ride on as well as over two hundred cars. My grandparents bought this property when my dad was a boy and they've added on as the years and finances permitted. Now, we are one of the biggest single-story buildings around, I believe. Definitely the biggest in Carrington Springs.

I park in the employee parking. Mom and Dad's brown VW van they've driven since I was a toddler is already here, which is not shocking. The people do not sleep.

I walk into the kitchen entrance and Mom is already greasing pans and making the lists on the giant chalkboards that hang on the wall. Across the top of it is written *Happy Birthday Ashten* in my Mom's perfectly straight handwriting.

Lovely. So much for me getting through today quietly.

"Ashten!" Grandma Minnie walks past me, already covered in flour. It's 5:03 in the morning. Much too early to already be covered in flour.

"Hi Grandma."

"Happy birthday, darling." She crushes me to her chest and pats my head.

Grandma Minnie is neither tall nor short, skinny or large. She just kind of *is*. She's got short, curly hair that used to be brown like mine but now is completely white. Anyone who knew Grandma Minnie as a younger woman immediately has to tell me how much I look like her when she was my age. I've seen the pictures. I can kind of see the resemblance, but I think it's the curls that make everyone think I look more like her than I really do.

"Ashten!" Mom hurries over and hugs me as well. Mom, on the other hand, is a little bit on the heavier side. This is what happens after thirty-five years of eating Grandma Minnie's rolls. I'm not sure my mother got a choice in what her life's work would become – she married Dad and married his family and their restaurant with him.

"Hello, hello," I say, wriggling out of their grasp. "Yes, I am here."

"Happy birthday, baby," Mom says. "I can't believe that you are thirty-one years old!" Mom is patting my cheeks and then swiping at her eyes.

Mom has been a little emotional lately. I imagine it has something to do with my younger brother getting married.

"Thirty-one." Dad appears out of thin air behind Mom and I can almost smell the disappointment radiating off of him. He heaves this huge sigh and then gives me a hug and pats my head like his mother just did. "Thirty-one. No husband, no children."

Mom rolls her eyes. "Lloyd. Please. It's her birthday. At least stop irritating her for this one day."

Dad sighs again. "Thirty-one," he moans again. "This is a birthday she should be celebrating surrounded by her husband and children."

Behold, my birthday greeting from my father for the past decade.

At one point, I told Dad that the average age a woman got married these days was 27.

Now, I keep my mouth shut and hope Dad has forgotten that fun little fact.

"Now, Lloyd," Mom chides again.

"What? I am only saying the truth. She needs a husband. She needs children. Who will take care of her when she is old? Not us, Margaret. We will be dead. Who will care for this restaurant that has been loving built from the ground up?"

"Oh for Pete's sake," Mom says, rolling her eyes.

Grandma Minnie backhands my father's shoulder and pats my head again.

The curls must be really out of whack today. Everyone is confusing me for a poodle.

"Well, good news, Dad. Will is going to be getting married in a few months and he can carry on the family legacy."

Dad sighs. "Lord, have mercy if your brother is the sole owner of this place."

"Please. You've been conditioning him to take this place over since he was six years old."

"Yes, and do you see the woman he is marrying? What am I even saying? She is not a woman, she's barely old enough to not be forced to order off the kid's menu."

"Dad." I'm rolling my eyes.

"Lloyd!" Mom is aghast. "You cannot say these things! She is a nice girl."

Dad is shaking his head. "She's too young. She doesn't care about the restaurant."

"She'll come around," Mom says. "I did. Beside, Everley is good for Will."

"And that's another thing. Who names their kid 'Everley'? It's a fake name."

"It's not a fake name."

"It's not a strong, normal name."

"Says the man who named his daughter 'Ashten'," I tell him.

Dad looks over at me, surprised. "Ashten is a wonderful name. It's your great-great-grandmother's maiden name."

Technically, it was *Ashton*. But my mother won was what probably the only round of her whole life and got to change the *o* to an *e* because it supposedly looks more feminine.

"Regardless, I like her," Mom says.

"So do I," Grandma Minnie says and immediately the conversation is over.

My grandmother has this thing that it's her restaurant and her rules and God forbid you argue or you will find yourself looking for a new job.

"How's Grandpa today?" I ask.

Grandpa John is not in the best of health anymore. He doesn't make it here by five. Usually, it's closer to six before he comes in.

"He's fine, he's fine," Grandma says, waving her hand. Grandpa could be dying of lung disease and all we would hear about is how fine he was. Grandma is smack in the middle of that generation that doesn't tell things to their offspring.

"Now, Ashten, you go get yourself a birthday cup of coffee."

I have been alive for thirty-one years. These people have all known me for all thirty-one of those years. I've been working with them for about twenty of those years. And I have never enjoyed a cup of coffee once in all those thirty-one years. Not once. Not even the nasty "coffee milk" my cousin feeds her babies while they are still attached to sippy cups.

But, this is like sacrilege to this family. Wadeleys drink coffee.

The older I get, the more convinced I am that I'm adopted.

If it weren't for the curly hair and the family resemblance, I'd be checking my birth certificate with a closer eye.

I obediently go over to the coffeemakers, if for no other reason than to leave my dad and his sighs and shaking of the head over my lack of a legacy I'm leaving here.

The coffeemaker is gurgling happily, getting ready for the first of the customers to show up at 5:30. Usually there is a line waiting outside the door, especially on Fridays and Saturdays.

I look at the coffee dripping into the carafe and I shake my head.

It's my birthday, I do not want to drink the coffee, so I will not drink the coffee. My cousin, Jacqueline, is busy processing oranges through our juicer, so I head over to her and she wordlessly hands me a glass.

"Happy birthday."

"Thanks."

She nods. Jacqueline isn't much for conversation unless it's in text message form.

Makes me crazy. Maybe I'm a part of that weird generation of millennials in the tiny window that was slightly too old when all this technology came out, but I much prefer face to face. Too many things get misconstrued over texts that never would in person.

 I take my juice and go review the specials of the day. Ever since my gig here became a summer position, I've been waitressing. There was a point in my life where I was in charge of some of the kitchen duties, but those days are gone.

Praise the Lord. I love cooking but I do not love cooking with forty-two eyes on my back and family pride resting in my incompetent hands.

There is a reason my grandmother's hands are as gnarled as they are – sixty-five years of legendary cooking and baking will do that to you.

The chalkboard is done and I sip my juice and memorize.

Friday's Menu:

Soup of the Day: Clam Chowder
Bread of the Day: Oatmeal Rye
Entrée of the Day: Salmon, Brown Butter Sauce,
Asparagus and Mashed Potatoes
Dessert of the Day: Sweet Potato Pie
Beverage of the Day: Raspberry Iced Tea

Breakfast never changes around here. We've got a huge assortment of baked goods, pancakes, egg dishes and lots and lots of coffee. People come and stay until lunch so they can finish up the Carb Load with Minnie's homemade rolls.

There's a reason I get home every night and run.

"So, whatever happened to that nice young man who was around here a lot?"

It's Dad and he's suddenly next to me, setting a giant cutting board down on a work table and getting to work trimming steaks, frowning at my glass of orange juice.

"What guy?"

"The one who ate his greens dipped in mayonnaise."

I smirk. Daniel would never live that down.

Good.

"Remember, Dad? He moved?"

To Anchorage.

Pretty sure there's never been a door more obviously slammed shut on a relationship than the one that reads

ANCHORAGE on the front of it. Even if I had wanted to move to Alaska, which I didn't, I sure wasn't going to move when we'd only been dating six months.

Add in the fact that he never actually asked me to move with so many words and we had a big fat red light in front of us.

I actually liked Daniel.

It was a hard few months afterward. Pretty sure my poor students thought I had completely lost it there.

Almost more than I liked Daniel, though, I liked the idea of knowing that there was *someone*.

Words I would never tell Katie. Mostly because I'd given her the exact opposite advice when she was floundering between men.

It's hard to follow your own wisdom, sometimes.

Dad is shaking his head. "Such a nice young man. Such a pity that he had such poor taste."

"Gee, thanks."

"For what?"

I smile because Dad doesn't even realize that he insulted his only daughter. "Nothing, it's okay."

Dad pats my arm and I'm immediately making a mental note to look into that blowout that my stylist was recommending last time she was trying to get a comb through my unending curls.

"You know, Ashten," she'd said, wiping sweat off her brow as she braced a foot on my back to balance herself while she fought with the comb, "They've come a long way with straightening techniques."

Too much patting going on around here. Either I'm looking incredibly poodle-like or everyone is in mourning for my birthday.

Probably some of both.

"You'll find someone, Ashten. But maybe you need to start going to new places. Is there no one at that new church you started going to?"

I shake my head. "Not really." The only decent single guy I'm aware of is Luke and he's not going to be single for too long, if I've read the writing on the wall correctly.

I give it two months before there's a solitaire on Katie's hand.

Maybe three.

Not that I would have been interested in Luke even if Katie wasn't in the picture.

Every so often, there's those quizzes that come around on Facebook and I'll occasionally get suckered into the ones that are along the lines of *Discover What Your Future Husband Will Be Like!* Usually it's late at night and I'm killing time in my room while Luke and Katie are baking cookies or having a Chinese takeout picnic in the living room or something equally as adorable and nauseating.

One time they came in carrying vases from a pottery class they took together.

Eliza, our good friend who lives across the street, and I often make fun of them.

Or at least we used to. Now Eliza is engaged to a guy who lives in St. Louis and she's too busy going on canvas painting dates of her own to smirk with me.

And here I am.

Getting lectured by my father.

According to the quizzes, though, I'm going to be here for awhile. Apparently my future husband resembles none other than *Mr. Darcy*.

Of course.

I'm sorry, but I have yet to meet Colin Firth anywhere recently.

But praise the Lord. I was worried at first that the quizzes would match me with Mr. Bingley.

God help us all, if that match happened. He's way too cheerful. I'd have to plant a garden like poor Charlotte when she married Mr. Collins just so I could get some time to myself and send my husband out there to dig. And I don't plant gardens that live. One time, Grandma Minnie gave me a succulent that was supposed to be idiot-proof and even monkeys could grow the thing.

I killed it in three weeks.

A new world record, if my research was correct. I thought about applying to the Guinness World Record people but it seemed like a lot of hassle for a dead plant.

"Anchorage?"

I blink back to Dad and his meat-trimming.

Sounds like we are going back to Daniel.

"Yep."

"I mean, Anchorage wouldn't be so bad. I've heard it's pretty. And I bet you could convince him to move back here when he hears about our benefits package."

"We have a benefits package?"

"Only for full-time employees."

News to me.

"Dad, that was almost a year ago, first off. I'm sure Daniel has moved on. And second, I don't want to move to Anchorage, even if it's just for a little while. What about my students? What about you guys?"

Dad rolls a shoulder, hands covered in raw meat. "I'm sure we could survive without you, Ashten. We do for nine months out of the year when you are teaching."

"Even so." The answer is no. I don't want to get into something with my dad on my birthday, but he's going to have to recognize that Fitzwilliam Darcys don't grow on trees around here.

We have enough trees that you'd think it would be possible, but nope. I've checked.

I've even written down a list of Mr. Darcy's personality traits so I can recognize him sooner.

Recognizes fine eyes.

Good at backhanded compliments.

Has an annoying aunt.

I mean, it's hard to find a decent single man, period, but a single man who is in possession of good fortune and those qualities is going to be basically impossible.

"I just want you to be happy, honey."

I look at my dad and it's my turn to pat his shoulder. "I am, Dad. Really."

"Really?" The look in Dad's eyes tells me he doesn't believe me, so I put as much emphasis into it as I can.

"*Really.*"

Maybe if I say it enough, I'll convince even myself.

CHAPTER *Two*

There's seriously nothing like a cold Coke after a long day at the restaurant.

I pop the top on the can, settling on Katie's overstuffed couch and take a long swig, closing my eyes.

Yes.

I've been doing this for as long as I can remember, which means my insides are probably toast, considering what a can of Coke can do to a rusted truck. A few years ago, I had to switch to caffeine-free because I was keeping myself up all night from the caffeine shot right before bed.

I lean back into the couch and close my eyes, holding the can with both hands.

"You are just weird."

I don't even open my eyes. "Hey Eliza."

"Hey." She closes the door behind her and I look up as she settles on the other sofa. "Long day?"

"Mm. I'm not used to the restaurant days anymore."

She grins and tosses a small gift bag over to me. "Well. Happy birthday. Sorry you had to work the whole day."

"You didn't need to get me anything."

"Well, that's good, because I didn't. It's definitely re-gifted."

24

I grin.

Inside the bag is a folded up piece of paper.

Join Us for the 16th Annual Library Day!

"What is this?"

"It's Library Day."

"I can see that. What is Library Day? It sounds like something a PBS Kids character would do."

Eliza's jaw falls open. "You've never heard of Library Day?" She is aghast.

"Um. No."

"Dude! It's the best! It's like this thing where everyone goes to the Carrington Springs Library and reorganizes all the books."

I look at her. "What?"

"Yeah. It's awesome. You get to make sure everything is still all organized and stacked correctly and all those Dewey Decimals are lined up straight."

"Don't we employ people for this?"

"Psh. This is Carrington Springs, Ashten. We barely have volunteers."

"You're seriously giving me a certificate to go organize library books for my birthday?"

"Yes, I am. It sounds amazing. And I'm in shock that you've never heard of it." Eliza shakes her head. "I only wish I could go too."

"No, you don't." Eliza is many things but I'm not sure that super organized and loves to read are on the list of her qualifications.

She grins. "You're right. I don't. I'm actually really thankful that I have to work that day. Bummer, man." She goes around the kitchen counter and pulls a mug out the cabinet, sticking it into the Keurig. Eliza and Katie love their coffee at any time of the day.

I've come in at three in the afternoon and found both of them sitting there with a mug in front of them. It's just weird, if you ask me. A Coke or an iced tea would be way more refreshing.

They keep telling me it's all about the warm mug in their hands, but it doesn't work for me.

If I'm drinking something hot, you should go ahead and cancel my week's plans, because I'm most likely deathly ill.

"So who gave you the Library thing?" I ask.

"What?"

"You said this was a re-gift."

"Oh yeah. Mike did. He said maybe then I could find some books outside of the *Calvin and Hobbes Anthology*."

I grin. "Won't he be annoyed when you don't go?"

"Nope. I'm working."

"You haven't worked nights in awhile."

"Every so often, there's a shift need that comes up."

"Why do I get the feeling that you were asking about the shift need?"

Eliza grins and returns to the couch, steaming mug in hand. "Where's Katie?"

"I hear your change of subject. She's out with Luke."

Eliza rolls her eyes. "Is it Katie or Luke who is the slow mover here?"

"What do you mean?"

"I mean, it's been almost a year. And she's not getting any younger. You'd think if they'd know something by now."

"Know what?"

"If they were going to get married. My mom used to say that if you don't know there's the potential after the third date, you have no business continuing to date."

I wish I'd met Eliza's mother. It sounds like she was a really wise woman.

I shrug. "I don't know."

"I mean, for goodness' sakes. I'm the one who's the holdout and look."

Eliza's ring shimmers in the lamp light.

"It's really beautiful." I sip my Coke and nod to my friend. She doesn't even notice.

Eliza holds her hand out, a small smile flirting around her mouth. Eliza and Cooper have known each other since Eliza was born, basically. He's adorable. Totally, head over heels in love with my friend. And now that she's finally

27

come around to admitting it, she's so cute to watch around him.

"Did you guys set a date yet?"

Eliza nods. "November. The Saturday before Thanksgiving."

"Nice."

"Yeah. I think it will work out."

"Is he moving here?"

Cooper lives in St. Louis. I don't know much about marriage, but I feel like it's probably best when the husband and wife live in the same town.

Eliza groans. "I don't know."

"Sounds like fun."

"Here's the thing," she says, sipping her coffee. "I love my job, I love my house and I love this town."

"And Cooper hates it all?"

"No, Cooper loves his job too."

"Ah."

Eliza sighs. "So, the question is who gets to give up their dream job."

"Sounds like a fun decision to make." I sip my Coke and I'm suddenly pretty thankful I'm single. At least my crazy is contained to one person. I can't imagine if I was trying to coordinate the school year and then the summer with someone else.

"So, are you going to do it?"

"Do what?" I ask.

"The Library thing."

"I think I could probably find enough to organize around here. But thanks."

"Come on, Ash. You know you would enjoy it. Plus, you're making Katie crazy by constantly redoing the kitchen."

I sigh. When I moved in here, Katie kept the spoons about as far away from the bowls as she could get them. Apparently, I am the only person who thinks it makes sense to make the morning cereal as stress-free as possible to consume.

"It's not my fault she was organizing everything wrong."

"Ash."

I roll my eyes. "Fine! I'll go. But only for a minute."

Eliza grins. "That's fine."

"Why do you want me to go so badly?"

"I think you'll like it."

I shake my head. "You know it sounds terrible. Why do you want me to go?"

She shrugs. "I heard through the grapevine that a lot of Carrington Spring's eligible bachelors are going to be there."

I make a face. "Why?"

"I don't know. Because there's nothing else to do in this town?"

"Not the best argument from someone trying to make her fiancé move here."

She grins. "I didn't say I minded it."

"Besides, I'm fairly certain that we don't have any bachelors here, eligible or not. If we did, my dad would have already set us up."

Eliza nods. "True. Well, anyway, it doesn't hurt to try. Wear your skinny jeans and your boots."

"Yes ma'am."

"And no offense to your current just-got-electrocuted look you have going on, but I like when your hair is mostly down and you pull back the front a little bit behind your ears. So you should do that."

I poke a finger into my bun that started fairly controlled and apparently has slowly deteriorated through the day.

Curly hair problems. People like Eliza have no idea. Eliza is one of those people who's hair is perfectly straight even on days where the humidity is in the ninetieth percentile.

Sickening.

"Anything else?" I ask, rolling my eyes.

She grins. "Cooper always compliments me the most when I'm wearing the food perfumes, so you probably can't go wrong with that."

"Food perfumes."

"Right. Like the Caramel Chocolate stuff from Bath and Body Works."

"That's sad."

"I'm waiting for someone to finally realize this and make sprays that smell like tacos or something."

I grin. "That might signal the end. Surely that's in Revelation. The day I mist myself to smell like a taco is the day I've officially given up. I'd rather be single."

The door bursts open right then and Katie appears, red-cheeked and out of breath, smiling so wide she can barely fit through the doorway.

I know what she's going to say before she exclaims it, so I think I'm tearing up before she even opens her mouth.

"I'm engaged!" she shouts, running inside.

Eliza and I are immediately off the couch, jumping, dancing, squealing, begging for her hand so we can make all the appropriate oohs and ahhs over the solitaire.

"Oh friend!" I wrap Katie in a hug and pull her close.

Katie, more than anyone, has always gotten me. We haven't even been friends that long in the grand scheme of things, but I feel like she knows me better and I know her better than almost anyone.

She grins at me, eyes sparkling, blonde hair all windblown.

"So? How? What? When?" Eliza is still half-jumping up and down. "Come on, Katie, you're the writer! Give us the deets!"

She laughs. "He took me up to that big hill at the edge of town—"

"The one overlooking the dump?" Eliza's forehead is wrinkling.

"Other end of town."

"The one overlooking that scrap metal factory?" I ask. So far, this is not sounding worthy of all those jumps I just made.

"No, no, not that one either."

I can't tell from Eliza's face that we are both having trouble coming up with the hill Katie is talking about.

She waves her left hand and the diamond glitters. "Anyway, it doesn't matter. He took me to the top of the hill and told me he loved me and he got down on one knee and sang me a song about how much he loves me and we are engaged!"

I give her another big hug and smile really big but inside, I'm shaking my head. Of course Luke would propose with a song. The man has a huge career out here because he sounds like a much-better-looking, if not sort of nerdy Michael Buble.

Who wears cardigans.

I wonder if he was wearing a cardigan tonight?

Sorry, but there should be some sort of rule that you can't propose to someone if you are wearing a cardigan.

Good gracious, what if he had the ring in the cardigan pocket?

I blink and force myself back to the present where Katie and Eliza are still laughing and dancing and the talk has obviously turned to the wedding.

"I'll get the coffee going!" Eliza shrieks and runs for the kitchen. "Planning starts now!"

Katie starts laughing and turns to me. "Oh Ashten! It's your birthday! Hold the coffee, Eliza. We need to focus on Ashten today."

"Are you kidding me?" I wave a hand. "You have lost your mind. So I turned a year older. Big whoop. Let's get down to wedding planning business. Commence the coffee, Eliza," I tell her and she unfreezes from where she had paused halfway to the fridge to refill the Keurig with the filtered water.

"Dude, you are so early nineties," Eliza says. "'Big whoop' is officially out. Has been for like two decades."

"Well, that's whack."

Katie can't stop giggling. "Oh Ashten."

I grin.

I pull my big quilt over my legs and halfway up my chest, snuggling down and reaching for my Bible on the bedside table. Grandma Minnie always told me that it's best to wake up with Jesus. "It's the only way to start the day," she would tell me, over and over.

I have tried I don't know how many times to get up early and read, but no matter what time it is, I cannot focus first thing. I'm not one of those people who pops out of bed at four and is instantly ready to absorb something I'm reading, like my grandmother is.

But I figure Jesus is probably okay with me reading at night too.

Hopefully, anyway.

I am going through a devotional book and reading through Hebrews. I do my lesson for the day and then read the last verses in chapter four.

Therefore, since we have a great high priest who has passed through the heavens, Jesus the Son of God, let us hold fast our confession. For we do not have a high priest who cannot sympathize with our weaknesses, but One who has been tempted in all things as we are, yet without sin. Therefore let us draw near with confidence to the throne of grace, so that we may receive mercy and find grace to help in time of need.

I look at the end of the chapter and something about those last few lines sticks out to me. I know I have read this chapter several times before, but for some reason, something about those words seems different tonight.

I have that Bible app on my phone where I can read the same passage in a bunch of different translations and so I quickly look it up in a few other ones.

Let us then approach God's throne of grace with confidence, so that we may receive mercy and find grace to help us in our time of need.

I look at the words.

Let us approach the throne of grace with confidence.

What did that even mean?

CHAPTER *Three*

I'm standing in the middle of a completely packed restaurant, pen poised, watching the people at the table all give the evil eye to the poor guy who was apparently too busy talking to actually be bothered with reading the menu while I was busy getting all their drinks.

"Oh man. This is a huge menu. Are you sure you guys don't need more time?" he asks.

"We all already ordered, Jerry."

I can't remember the last time I heard such a glacial tone.

"Take your time," I tell him, trying to instill some warmth in my voice so I can maybe start melting the verbal icicles being thrown like javelins toward the slow reader. "It is a large menu."

"How about a burger," the guy finally says, gasping. "With fries."

I don't even bother asking him which of our twelve burger choices he wants. I'll come up with his order on my own. I have a feeling that he'll be thankful to eat at this point.

I nod and gather the menus. "We'll have that right out. Meanwhile, I think Tim is going around with Minnie's famous rolls." I nudge the stack of plates and basket piled high with tiny paper cups full of our homemade honey butter, which is honestly about eighty percent powdered sugar.

People don't come to Minnie's to eat healthy.

"Thanks."

I drop the menus off with my cousin, Tanya, who is one of the hostesses today and go to the back to put in the order for the table. A ten top is a pretty normal sized group for one o'clock on a Sunday.

Yesterday was my day off and I decided to play hooky for the Bible study I usually go to on Saturday mornings and sleep in. Probably not my most shining moment, but Katie and Eliza kept me up until past two talking about wedding plans and I'd been up since before five. They were Pinteresting wedding décor and I was googling "can you die from sleep deprivation" on my phone under the table.

Turns out you can.

After I finally woke up, I did laundry. And ate tortilla chips and salsa for lunch. And then again for dinner because I was all alone in the house since Katie was on a date and when I texted Eliza to see if she wanted to go get dinner with me, she was also on a date.

Basically, yesterday was a wash.

Here's the thing. I'm so excited for my friends.

So I feel bad being so over the fact that I'm the only one who is single.

"Ashten, order up!"

I shove my order book in my apron, grab a tray and head to the counter where my brother, Will, is throwing sweet potato fries on plates and yelling at the cook.

"I need a double patty melt on a multigrain!"

My order is off to the side and Will looks over at me as I load it onto a tray.

"Are you coming to the family dinner tonight?"

I shrug. "I don't know. Probably." Odds are good the alternative is sitting in an empty house. Cooper is probably going to be back in St. Louis tonight, so Eliza might be free. But you never know.

Plus, it's Sunday night. If I don't show up to Family Dinner, Dad would send people to start checking the morgues.

"You know that Dad is expecting you to come."

"I know." Most likely means more lectures on how unhappy I am.

"Everley would really like you to be there too." Will chucks a handful of baked Lays on an empty plate.

I nod. "I'll do my best."

Will's fiancée is one of those people who is kind of awkward to talk to. I don't know if it's her age or her personality or what it is, but we have absolutely nothing in common other than both being women with opposable thumbs.

So, I usually end up telling her stories about the olden days and she smiles all politely and then tells me how funny I am while she's not laughing at the punch lines.

It's great fun.

Not.

Good night, I am stuck in the nineties.

I take the order out to the table, refill drinks, write down more orders and take more out. The short day goes by quickly and I'm helping close up before I've had the chance to sit down the entire day.

Suddenly, I'm starving.

Dad looks at me as he pockets his keys to the restaurant as we walk to the parking lot. "You are coming, right?" He says it like a question, but I know it's not.

"I'm coming." Might as well get a good dinner in. I'm not sure my esophagus can take another night of chips and salsa.

Heartburn is such an old person problem to have.

"Good. Everley is going to be there." I can hear the eye-rolling in his tone.

Poor Dad. He's not a fan of Will's choice of a future wife.

And poor Everley. She has to deal with my so-not-subtle father over the dinner table every time she dares to come over.

I think Dad looks at my brother's skinny, fairly timid and shy fiancée and gets all freaked out about this girl making the decisions for his future and the future of the business he's dedicated his life to. But Will is nothing short of bossy, and obnoxiously so. Even if Everley is like the world's worst boss, Minnie's will do just fine, thanks to Will and his Iron Fist.

Mom and Grandma Minnie left the restaurant a couple of hours ago to get dinner stuff going. It's just me and Dad closing up, the parking lot is empty. Sunday is the one day we open late and close early. Apparently, we used to be closed the whole day and then Grandma Minnie started feeling like the folks who lived in Carrington Springs without any family around needed a place to come for Sunday dinner. So, we are open from eleven to four.

"Are you sure you aren't interested in anyone?" Dad bursts as we get to the cars.

"Dad."

"No, no, I know. I'm so worried for you, honey. What if you never get married?"

I mean, the thought has crossed my mind too. What if I am always the fifth wheel? What if Katie and Eliza get married and there's still no one? What if they start having kids and I morph from the friend to the babysitter? What if I become like Mary in *Pride and Prejudice* and I spend my days reading and playing the piano in my parents' house for the rest of my life?

I mean, the reading part sounds nice, but the piano and my parents' house doesn't sound exactly like the American Dream.

Maybe that's why *Pride and Prejudice* was based in England.

When my thoughts start turning into these kind of things, it's usually time for bed.

"Dad," I start and he holds up a hand, cutting me off.

"Let's put it to rest. Let's put it to rest," he says. I can't decide if he's speaking to himself or to me, since he's the one who brought it up.

"Okay."

"I'll see you at the house."

I climb in my car and follow Dad to the house I grew up in. It's the house next door to my grandparents. And the house on the other side of my grandparents is where my uncle Jacob and his family live.

I wasn't kidding when I said that Mom married Dad and his entire family and their business. She basically married him knowing that she was never going to be alone ever again.

It sounds miserable.

Don't get me wrong, I love my family. I seriously have the best family in the whole world. But there's something to be said for time alone to think every so often.

The street is packed with cars like it usually is on Sunday nights. I finally find a bare patch of curb eight houses down and it takes me a good ten minutes to parallel park.

I would be lying if I said I haven't parked in the middle of the street before, handed my keys to someone walking down the road and asked them to parallel park my car for me.

Thankfully, they didn't just drive off and they really did park the car.

I have no idea how I passed this test in Driver's Ed.

My grandparents house is gigantic. I think I remember hearing that it's over five thousand square feet and it's beautiful. They built it themselves when my dad was a little kid. It's made for huge family dinners.

You can hear the noise from outside the door.

I take a deep breath and go inside.

Right away, I see four uncles, about eight cousins and my Grandpa John.

"Ashten!" Grandpa exclaims and pulls me over to kiss my head.

Grandpa John is moving a lot slower these days, but aside from the speed and his more white than gray hair, he's the exact same as he was twenty years ago. He's super tall, over six feet and has the most amazing Tom Selleck-ish moustache.

He would be kind of an imposing character if you didn't know how soft he is inside.

"How's my girl?" he asks, squeezing my shoulders.

I'm so thankful for my grandfather. Where Dad and I have some weirdness between us, Grandpa John has always understood me like very few people ever have.

"I'm okay," I tell him.

He gives me a look. "Not doing well?"

"Just busy. I'm tired." And I am. I usually have to be up early to go teach, but restaurant early is a different kind of early.

Plus, I don't know. I feel...unmotivated. Maybe that's it. Like this is all pointless.

I don't know how to put it into words.

The chaos is erupting around us and Grandpa John squeezes my shoulders again. "Sounds like we need to have a little Grandpa and Ashten date, hmm?"

I smile. "That would be great, Grandpa."

"Okay. Well, go get a roll from Grandma. Those can cure almost everything."

"Except my waistline."

Grandpa John rolls his eyes. "You are lovely, Ashten and don't you ever say anything that diminishes that. To do so only insults the God who made you."

I love my grandpa.

I smile.

"Go get a roll. And tell Grandma that if I'm barbecuing, I need the meat."

"Yes sir."

I head into the kitchen, where I know Grandma will be. If she's not cooking at the restaurant, she's cooking here at home. The woman lives in the kitchen.

I asked her about it one time and she told me that she loved being in the kitchen because it's where she felt close to God. "I create in here, Ashten. I think. I knead and pray. I feel myself come alive when I am mixing or pouring or crafting a new recipe. And I feel God here. He is near to me in the kitchen."

Now, she's pulling a giant cookie sheet that is discolored and stained with age from the oven, rows of puffy, golden brown rolls on it, filling the whole house with their yeasty aroma.

Grandma is talking to my cousin Kit and she's shaking her head at me.

I have no idea why. Then Grandma turns and I see she's sporting a new apron.

It's got a picture of a roll on it and underneath it says, *My buns bring all the boys to the kitchen, y'all.*

I blink at Kit and she keeps shaking her head, like a broken bobble head doll.

"Hi. Hi Grandma."

"Ashten, hello, sweetheart."

"Nice, uh, apron."

More head shaking. Kit has to be getting a headache.

"Oh, thank you, dear. Your cousin Vince gave it to me. Isn't it the truth?"

"Uh, yeah, I guess it is."

Vince. Figures it was him. Looks like I'll be having a chat with him. You don't dress your completely oblivious grandmother in something like that.

I mean, that has to be Biblical somewhere.

"Grandpa said he needs the meat."

"Your mother took it outside."

"Okay. Grandpa is still inside."

"Well, that won't go well, considering your mama refuses to learn how to use a grill." Grandma Minnie rolls her eyes but she has a warm, soft smile on her face.

Grandma Minnie and Grandpa John had four boys. My dad is the oldest. I've heard story after story about what they were like growing up and it was basically insanity in this house.

So when my dad married my mom, she became the daughter my Grandma Minnie had always longed for. And she was the only daughter-in-law for three years, until my Uncle Jim married Aunt Hannah. Mom and Grandma Minnie were, and are, tight.

In a lot of ways, Grandma Minnie also became the mother my mom had always longed for. Mom doesn't talk about her parents too often. They died when I was in high school, I think. I'd only met them a couple of times that I actually remember. I asked one time why we never saw them and Mom kind of stroked back my hair and told me that we'd talk about it later.

We never did.

I don't even remember the last time I thought about them.

We were with Grandpa John and Grandma Minnie almost every single day, so there was never really a moment to miss my other grandparents. If we weren't at the restaurant, Grandma would stop by with some cookies or rolls or Grandpa would be by with candy canes or something else that would make my mom roll her eyes, but we all knew she secretly didn't mind. She would get this little smile on her face and we knew it was a big act.

Mom comes back in the kitchen then. "Hi honey."

"Hi Mom. Did Grandpa find you?"

"Yes. He's got the meat going. I didn't see you much at the restaurant today. How did everything go?"

Today was a blur. Short days usually are.

"Good," I nod. "Same as the usual."

"How are Katie and Eliza?"

Mom has met them a few times. They come into Minnie's for cinnamon rolls fairly often and she's come to my house a few times.

"Katie is engaged," I tell Mom quietly. Best if my dad doesn't know this. First, because it will remind him of my current relationship status. Second, because he will start panicking over my impending move into his house.

I haven't lived with my parents in eight years, but anytime a roommate gets married, Dad immediately begins a woe-is-me parade at the loss of his Man Cave.

Which, interestingly enough, used to be my room.

I need to find out when Katie is kicking me out of her house. I'm about five months away from having a down payment for a house of my own saved up. Assuming she is aiming for post-Christmas wedding, I should be fine.

Mom's eyes get wide. "Really. Luke finally proposed?"

"Finally." Mom knows all about my thoughts on the Katie and Luke thing. Mr. Rogers never moved very fast either though. Maybe it's a cardigan thing.

You don't see people running in them too often.

"How are you doing with that?" Mom asks.

"I'm excited for her." And I truly am. Katie has wanted to get married her whole life. I'm so happy it's finally happening for her.

Mom gives me a look, the same look I've gotten for the past six or so years. The kind that says, "Oh, poor Ashten. She's so lonely and sad."

I'm not lonely or sad.

Am I?

I'm really not. I'm too busy to be lonely or sad. Usually at the end of the day, the only emotion I feel is exhaustion.

Occasionally hungry. If hungry can be considered an emotion.

But only after my days in the classroom. No one leaves Minnie's hungry. It's the restaurant motto.

And it includes the staff.

Mom pats my arm. "Well. Congratulations to Katie. Help me make the salad."

I pull out the cutting boards while Mom gets the vegetables from Grandma's fridge. Grandma is one of those people who always has the fixings for anything you could possibly want to make. Chocolate chip cookies? Got it. Omelets? Done. Chicken fried steak? Given.

So, when Mom reappears from the depths of the fridge with about eight different varieties of vegetables, I'm not shocked at all. Plus, I'm willing to bet that at least half are homegrown.

48

I have no idea how my grandmother manages to do everything she does.

There's a terrible smell filling the kitchen right now, though, and I wrinkle my nose, trying to be polite about it, because you don't start declaring your grandmother's kitchen disgusting.

"Oh my goodness, what is *that*?" Mom asks, covering her nose with her hand.

Or, maybe my mother does.

Grandma rolls her eyes. "Some customer at the diner told Grandpa that the best cure for seasonal arthritis is to eat a hard boiled egg every morning for the two months before the season starts."

Mom and I look at her.

"Seriously?" Mom asks.

"Really?" I ask at the same time.

Grandma waves a knife at us. "You know John. And yes. And now my fridge will smell like death forever, because there is no worse smell than cooling hard boiled eggs."

"Why don't you get the pre-cooked and peeled eggs for him?" Mom says. "Then you don't have to smell them all the time."

Sometimes I get so wrapped up in my own stuff that I never stop to think about other people. I have it so good. Yes, I am tired. Yes, I work hard. Yes, I am apparently going to be alone because I don't think I will ever find anyone who I could see myself spending my life with. But goodness. It could be so much worse.

I could work in the factory that sells those pre-cooked and peeled eggs.

God forbid.

You would probably smell like this forever.

Grandma Minnie shrugs. "At this point in our lives, I let him do what he wants to do."

Mom shakes her head. "Well. Do you want me to put an egg in the salad?"

"Why not? Then we can all avoid arthritis."

I grin.

Mom slices the cucumbers and tomatoes, I start chopping the lettuce and dicing the red onions and zucchini. We add the egg, some cheddar cheese and I find a few slices of ham in the fridge. In no time, we have a gourmet salad on our hands.

Grandpa John returns with the sizzling meat and starts the chorus of "DINNER'S READY!" that echoes through the house like I always imagined people used to do in the olden days when a town messenger would appear.

We all find our seats around the different tables in three different rooms and Grandpa and Grandma hustle around setting portions of each part of the dinner in the middle of each of the tables. We used to offer to help and always got shut down, so now, we wait to be served. Grandpa goes to his seat and prays and it's the only minute of the whole night where the house is basically quiet.

The second he says "amen", the quiet is gone and a roaring cacophony takes it's place.

I look around the tables, at all these people I'm related to somehow.

Everyone is talking, everyone is laughing or debating or making some sort of conversation. Little kids are telling jokes or playing with their food and the parents are shushing or scolding and it's like everyone here knows their place.

I mean, even Will's fiancée seems to be enjoying herself.

I should remember to go at least say hi. I didn't even see them come in.

But, there's this feeling deep in my chest. And it grows and swells and expands until I feel like there isn't enough room for my lungs to take a full breath.

I don't know where I fit anymore.

I get home and Katie is gone, probably out with Luke somewhere. It's still pretty early, but I've got a very early morning tomorrow, so I head to bed and pull my Bible on my lap.

Hebrews 4 has been in the back of my mind constantly.

Let us approach the throne of grace with confidence.

There's a little notation in my Bible that I wrote, but I don't remember writing, so I flip to the reference I'd written down. Ephesians 3:12.

...We have boldness and confident access through faith in Him.

So our faith in Christ gives us the confident access to the throne.

I reach over and turn off the light.

Confident access.

I don't think I've ever been truly confident in my whole life.

CHAPTER *Four*

It's Monday night. I'm sitting in my car, shaking my head, because it has come to this.

Library Day.

I can't believe I'm here. I totally should have told Eliza I'd come and stayed home instead.

Inevitably though, I would have read every single verse about telling the truth tonight in my Bible reading. It's how it works.

I sigh at the windshield and pocket my keys.

I'll stay for five minutes and then I'm going to waste the rest of the night at Starbucks. Because even though Eliza says she's working, I would bet she's going to be checking for my car to make sure I'm not home tonight.

The joy of being friends with someone across the street. Maybe I don't want to be looking for a house in the neighborhood.

I climb out of the car and walk into the basically empty library. An older lady with Aunt Bee's hairstyle is sitting at a desk inside the entrance and she looks up at me.

"Hello!" she says.

"Hi."

"Are you here for Library Night?"

My life is so lame now.

"Yes," I say.

She grins. "Your enthusiasm is contagious, my dear."

I immediately love this woman. "Sorry. A friend of mine is making me come." I look around the empty place and shake my head. "And apparently I'm the only one sad enough to be here."

"Oh no. There are quite a few of you! They are in the conference room getting the instructions."

So it looks like I'm not only lame, I'm also late.

Great.

I follow the lady's directions to the back conference room and there's about fifteen people in there. I sneak in the back and stand against the wall.

There's a guy who is far too skinny for his own good standing in the front, pointing to a diagram he has on a big white board explaining how the Dewey Decimal system works.

"So, then, you match up these numbers first and then you look at this decimal."

He's wearing a plaid shirt and jeans and everything is tucked in and belted in a way that makes him look even skinnier.

Poor guy. He's the definition of painfully thin.

Everyone is nodding around the room. I can only see the backs of people's heads, but it's weird to me that this is even a thing.

Library Day.

This is how you know you're in a small town. The fact that I haven't heard about Library Day is either proof that I used to not be lame or that it's been a long time since I've been in the library.

I'm a millennial. If I have time to read a book, I download it to my phone with the library app. The only library I consistently go to is the school library with my students.

"All right, so I think we are good. Does anyone have any questions?"

There's a general shaking of heads because millennials or not, we all typically grew up learning about the Dewey Decimal system at some point in our lives.

"Great! Thanks for coming to help and remember! This is fun!"

Right.

Everyone stands and I shrink back against the wall a little more so I can potentially blend into the crowd.

Ten minutes. I will stay for ten minutes and then I'm going home and changing into my sweatpants and getting myself a Coke. I don't even care if Eliza sees my car anymore.

Everyone files out of the room and I wait patiently so I can slide into the back of the line and quietly disappear from Library Day.

"Ashten?"

I look up and Eliza's brother, Mike, is standing right in front of me, looking about as awkward as I feel.

"Mike."

"Hey."

"Hi."

And there we stand. I give him one of those closed-mouthed smiles because my brain is completely failing me on anything remotely interesting to say.

"So, I didn't know you were coming to Library Day."

"I didn't know you were either," I say.

"Yeah," he says.

And then we stand there again. He shoves his hands into the pockets of his jeans and I'm working really hard to avoid eye contact.

He's not this hard to talk to when Eliza is around.

Or is he? I don't actually know if I've ever really talked to Mike. He seems, I don't know. Aloof? Grouchy? Annoyed? All of the above? I've only been around him a handful of times and I can't say he's made the best impression.

I know a little of Eliza's past and she and Mike didn't have the easiest time of it. He actually half-raised her. He's always been a little too overprotective of her and I know he makes her nuts half the time. She's super independent.

Then he moved here and freaked her out completely that she would never be allowed to make her own decisions again. But I guess it's going okay. She seems happy, anyway. But, then again, she's also engaged so maybe she's come to grips with the never making her own decisions again thing.

I was worried about her for awhile, though.

"Well," Mike says.

"Yeah," I nod.

We both file out of the conference room as well. I am assigned the "CRAFTS AND WOODWORKING" section of the library and I reorganize as fast as I can so I can leave.

It would seem that crafters are not very organized.

I mean, seriously. Is it that hard to look at a book and put it back where you found it? It's like a three year old did this section.

And honestly, I had no idea there were so many books about crafting. Or woodworking. Or crocheting.

I think Eliza can crochet and I know Katie has done her fair share of crafts, but for the life of me, I can't do anything. I can barely be in the same room as a glue gun without giving myself third degree burns.

I picked the wrong career. Almost every day, I do some sort of craft with my students. But usually, I can give them directions and let them loose and I don't have to actually craft anything. But really, the perk of elementary school is most of the crafts involve very little dexterity and nothing that could cause burns or puncture wounds, like I've had happen when I attempted sewing awhile back.

I pull a book off the shelf from the wrong place for it and start smirking at the title.

How To Make Gifts Without Scarring Yourself

Sounds like I need to check this book out.

"How's it going?" The skinny guy who should probably untuck his shirt is making the rounds and he pokes his head on my aisle. His eyes immediately get big when he sees the mountain of books that is trying to eat me.

"Oh fine, fine," I say, waving a hand.

"Are you okay? Do you need help?"

The only thing I need is to get out of here and go home. "No, no," I say, shaking my head quickly because heaven forbid I do this while also trying to be social. Eliza painted this as a great singles' place to meet. I'm seeing this as something I will be avoiding from this point on.

It would seem he's hard of hearing. "I'll get someone over here right away," he says, completely ignoring me and leaving.

Double time, Ashten, double time!

I start going as fast as I possibly can, shoving books into the shelves so that I don't have to sit here and try to make conversation with someone I've never met before.

"Here you go!" The guy is back. "Reinforcements! Plus, Dewey Decimals are always more fun with a friend!"

That is very much debatable. And based on the level of enthusiasm in his voice, he either is trying to help himself believe that or he is a new breed of weird.

He steps aside and Mike comes up behind him, looking oh-so-happy and excited to be here.

Not.

"Hi."

"Hi."

"Great!" Skinny Dude claps his hands together and gives us a cheesy, fake smile. "You guys have fun!" He leaves.

I could do without this kind of fun.

Mike is looking at me and the mountain of books with a mix of horror and pity and disdain and I feel about six inches tall. Possibly because he's standing and I'm on the floor, but still. He could have a nicer expression. Or at least iron out those frown lines between his eyebrows. If he keeps his expression too much longer, he's going to need to stop by Ulta next time he's in St. Louis so the nice people there can give him some kind of retinol or something to help him go back to looking like he's in his thirties again.

I don't see how two people who come from the same parents can be so different. Mike is grouchy and standoffish and sort of comes across as better-than-thou. Eliza is happy and fun and welcoming and the first time I met her, she gave

me this giant hug and told me we were going to be best
friends.

They are polar opposites. I mean, Eliza has laugh lines.
Mike has scowl lines.

"Well."

I nod. "Let's get it done."

We work in total silence for about three minutes and I
feel every single second of it. I've seriously been staring at
the spine of one book for ninety seconds because I can't get
my eyes to focus on the faded numbers on the label long
enough to read them.

And goodness knows I'm not putting this book in the
wrong spot. Not with him double checking everything I put
into the shelf.

I wish he would go away.

Maybe if I make some light conversation, this will go
faster and I can go home.

"So, how are you adjusting to Carrington Springs?" I
ask.

Mike shrugs. "Fine."

Well, I'm glad I can at least count on him helping me
pick up the slack in the conversational reins.

When I was in junior high, I was picked as "Most
Awkward To Talk To". It was a great thing to open and read
as a braced-teeth, pimply-faced kid who wanted to be left
alone with her Anne of Green Gables books. I feel like I've

60

become easier to talk to and better at keeping conversations going the older I get, but there's always going to be this twelve year-old me in the back of my mind who carries that awful badge.

It's not helping the whole "confidence" thing that I keep reading about in Hebrews.

If I can't even approach my friends or acquaintances with confidence, how in the world can I approach Jesus?

Or anyone?

Maybe it's that I'm just not very good with small talk.

Eliza is great at small talk. She excels at it. She loves it so much that she almost hates the deeper waters, which are way more comfortable for me. It's amazing we are friends. The only reason I can survive talking with her is that I've been honing my small talk skills at the restaurant and she's been coming out of her shell and going into the deep with me.

But obviously, there will be no friendship ahead for me and her brother.

Honestly, I would be happy if I never saw him again.

Maybe this could work. I'll obviously see him at Eliza's wedding, most likely. But weddings are crazy. And I'm a bridesmaid. So, I shouldn't have to talk to anyone because my job is to keep Eliza glowing and blissfully unaware of anything remotely wrong.

This can work.

We keep stacking books and I am very careful to stay on my side of the pile on the floor in the middle of us so I can say as little as possible to him. As much as I hate small talk, I hate awkward silence even more, so I am gritting my teeth together so I don't say something dumb.

I have made randomly spewing words into something of an art form.

Thus my badge of junior high honor, I guess.

Mike seems totally oblivious to the silence, either that or he's buckling down and trying to be done as quickly as humanly possible too.

As soon as I am done with this torture, I am driving straight to Minnie's and getting myself a double slice of chocolate cake. Or a slice of cake and a brownie. With ice cream. And a Coke.

A *regular* Coke.

And I'm charging it to Eliza.

Library Day is officially the worst gift I have ever been given.

I shove the last book in with a very satisfying *THUD* and I jump up off the floor. "Okay, well, goodbye!" I say in an overly loud, super shrill voice to Mike. I sound like an animated hamster who has a foot caught in the wheel.

"Leaving?"

Here's what I want to say: "Dude, I cannot get out of here fast enough."

Here's what I do say: "Yeah, sadly, I need to leave. I'll see you later, Mike."

"I think they were going to serve coffee after everyone was done," Mike says.

I raise a shoulder and smash my lips together in a half-hearted attempt to look sad about this. "Ah, that's too bad that I have to go. But it's okay. I hate coffee, so that works out. Okay, bye."

"Really?"

"Really. So I'll see you later." Hopefully not too soon. I think I've had my fill of awkwardness for the year. And I've now said some form of "goodbye" twelve times, so for goodness' sake, surely he can see that I want to leave already.

He nods. "Good-bye."

I get in the car and drive to Minnie's. They won't close for another hour, but this is definitely the slow time of the day. I opened, so I got to leave before the lull hit. Thankfully.

Plus, I can only do about eight hours before I am done with all people forever.

I walk inside and my cousin, Jamie, is standing by the hostess table, frowning at me.

"I thought you were off for the rest of the day?" he says, flicking a dish towel over his shoulder.

Jamie is one of those guys who will likely shape up to be a really nice looking man someday. But right now, he's so wiry and his hair is all scraggly and oily and his face is all scrungy from a combination of acne and not shaving super regularly. Grandpa is a big proponent of clean shaven faces out front, so Jamie is usually in the back.

But, all that aside, he might be nice looking. Someday. Potentially.

"I am off. I need cake."

Jamie looks at me. "A guy?"

"Maybe."

"Come with me."

I follow him into the back and he nods to the third of Grandma Minnie's Chocolate Chocolate Cake left on the counter.

This cake doesn't mess around. Not only is it chocolate cake, but the frosting is chocolate and there's a chocolate ganache in between the layers. This cake might be the only thing that could make me turn into a coffee drinker, and it would be purely to cut the sweetness.

Jamie already has me a Coke, though, so I take the glass with a thank you and pull up a barstool to the big working counter, slicing a medium size piece off the cake and putting the lid back on.

"How was the evening?" I ask, forking off a huge bite.

"Apparently better than yours."

"I went to Library Day."

"Is that like a PBS show or something?"

64

"Should have been. I guess it's where everyone shows up and reorganizes the books."

There are a couple of other people in the back, and two of my cousins and one of the other waitresses start laughing. My cousin, Tina, is unloading the dish sanitizer and shaking her head.

"You seriously went to that? Sorry, Ash, but that's like the definition of lame."

"If you need help meeting men, I can introduce you to some people." Kendra is the one person in the room right now who is not related to me. I think she's a friend of one of the cousins. She's been around forever.

Kendra shrugs at me. "The offer is on the table. I'm just saying. I know lots of people."

"Don't tell my dad that," I warn her.

Jamie is still frowning. "Wait, so the library thing was a singles' event? Seriously? Dude, this is why I can't wait until I can afford to leave this town."

Jamie has been talking about leaving since he was old enough to talk. So he went to school in Illinois but was right back at his parents' house after he graduated college. I have no idea why he is still here.

"You could go now," Tina says, rolling her eyes.

Tina and Jamie are the same age and always have had this weird sibling rivalry thing going even though they aren't siblings.

"Rent is expensive," Jamie says.

"I told you not to major in liberal arts," Tina says. "You could be making more than ten dollars an hour right now if you'd listened to me and majored in anything else."

"So, why are you still working here, if you're so smart?" Jamie shoots back. "Oh, that's right. Because you majored in Spanish. I can see how far it's carried you."

"Come on, guys, simmer down," I say.

"That's enough now," my cousin, Rachel, who has been quietly working on a pile of dishes up until now, says.

Jamie rolls his eyes. "Anyway."

"Anyway," Tina says, going back to unloading.

I finish my cake and take a few swallows of the Coke. I know it's not caffeine free, since Minnie's doesn't have that, so I'm going easy tonight. I would like to sleep since I'm going to be back here at five tomorrow.

Ugh.

"Well, I'm out," I say, carrying my plate over to the sink and rinse it so it doesn't create more work for Rachel. "Thanks for the dessert."

"See you tomorrow, Ashten."

"Bye, Ashten."

I leave and drive home. Katie's car is in the driveway, so I open the front door quietly, just in case she's already gone to bed.

The TV is tuned to HGTV and Katie is curled up under a blanket, holding a cup of coffee. She's got the little lamp on the end table on and the light over the sink, but otherwise, the house is dark and quiet.

"Hey friend!"

"Hi Katie."

I sit down on the other couch and look at my friend.

I don't understand how Katie has been single for so long. She's gorgeous, she's so sweet and generous and she's one of those people who loves Jesus with all her heart. I always feel like a sub-par person next to her.

Plus, she's got the most amazing hair.

And we've already discussed my hair.

Katie reaches for the remote and mutes the brothers who are demolishing a house. "How was your night?"

My brain quickly decides that it's best to not even mention that Mike was there. Then it will open up a whole new conversation and one I'm not really interested in having. Katie is right in the middle of the "I'm so happy and in love and everyone should feel this way" stage.

Singles: Beware the newly engaged. They make poor choices when high on diamond sparkles and tulle choices.

I downplay.

"It was fine." I watch the muted brothers on TV as they make a big deal about muscling an old fridge out of a house. They appear to be going on and on over this fridge and how heavy it is.

Maybe it's a slow broadcast day.

Either that or my dad is right and they really will put anything on TV these days.

He believes that all quality programming ended in the 80s.

Katie is looking at me and I realize she's waiting for me to expound on my original statement. Katie is one of those people who kind of waits people out. Plus, I think she's figured out that if she waits long enough, the awkward silence in the room gets to me and I start talking so the quiet will stop.

For being an introvert, you'd think I would appreciate the quiet. But no. There's a reason I became a grade school teacher. You get to control the amount of quiet in a classroom.

And honestly, with children, there is rarely quiet anyway.

I try to shrug my way out of it, but Katie just sips her coffee and waits.

Sometimes, I can't wait to have my own house. I can imagine coming home from an awkward night and not having to relive the whole entire thing all over again. I could put things out of my mind and not have to rehash them for an audience.

The door opens and Eliza comes in. Katie and I don't even look up.

"Saw you pull in," Eliza says to me and plops down next to Katie. She leans over and sniffs Katie's drink.

"Hazelnut?"

"Macadamia."

"Decaf?

"Yep."

Eliza is back off the couch and over at the Keurig as quickly as she sat down.

Eliza doesn't do things halfway or slow. I've never seen the girl still.

She's back with her coffee in less than a minute and she tucks her legs under herself, carefully holding her cup and sipping the hot liquid.

"I can smell the sugar from here," Katie says, frowning. "Goodness."

"Like you're one to talk."

"I probably use half of what you do."

"Sugar is sugar, my friend."

"Don't tell that to the people who panic over high fructose corn syrup."

Eliza grins at Katie. "So?" she asks me.

"So what?"

"Library Day!" Eliza grins. "How was it? Was it spectacular? I bet it was spectacular. You were there for a long time! Did you talk to anyone? Meet anyone? Are you going to go out for coffee with anyone now?"

"Will you just let her answer?" Katie asks, swatting at Eliza.

"I'm giving her a few talking points."

"She has plenty! Let the woman talk!"

I smirk and pull a pillow into my lap. These two are my favorites. I met them at a bowling alley, as weird as that is, but it was totally God destined. I was all upset and emotional because Will had stood me up and we were supposed to be discussing something that seemed really important at the time but now I don't even remember what it was. Anyway, these two showed up, invited me over and we all went out for dessert afterward.

"Anyway?" Eliza draws the word out, rolling her eyes and looking at me.

"I don't know. It was fine." The goal is to stick to my previous plan. The less I have to share, the better.

"Just fine? Did you know anyone there?" Eliza asks, all suggestively, because she obviously knows her brother was there.

I sigh.

Katie looks at Eliza. "Why? Was someone she knows there?"

"Mike went."

"Oh really?" Katie looks over at me. "Did you see Mike?"

"Yeah, I saw him."

This conversation needs to end. I can already see what Eliza is trying to do and it's not going to work. Besides, surely she knows her brother well enough to know that we would be the worst couple ever.

He's mean and I'm awkward.

We would be like meant to fail at life. We'd become That Couple who never gets invited anywhere because no one actually likes them. So we'd only get pity invitations for like Eliza and Katie's childrens' birthday parties. And then we would stand in the corner and scowl at people.

Not that I jump to harsh conclusions or anything.

Anyway. Aside from the dismal future, there needs to be some sort of spark or *something* and there is nothing but disdain from him. And nothing definitely nothing on my side either.

Eliza is all smiley and giggly and I have a feeling that this was her plan all along with my awful gift. "So, did you talk? Did you hang out across from the Dewey Decimal system? He's an awesome guy, isn't he? Katie, he's awesome, right?"

I think Katie can see what's going on now too and she shakes her head at Eliza. "Really?"

"What?"

"You sent her to Library Day to meet your brother? Could you not have had like a dinner party or something and introduced them that way instead?"

"Well, I didn't want to be too obvious."

Katie rolls her eyes.

Eliza looks at me and I sigh. "I mean, yes, I talked to him. But Lyzie, there's no way anything is happening there."

Eliza smiles a sweet smile. "Picked up the nickname, huh?"

You can only hang around Eliza and Cooper for so long before it becomes second nature. He only refers to her by Lyzie.

"I want you to be happy," Eliza says.

"I am happy," I tell her.

"No, I mean, I want you to be *really* happy," she says. "And Katie is engaged and I'm engaged and it seemed so perfect that you were single and Mike is single. I figured it was meant to be."

"Well, it's not. But thank you for thinking of me. And guys, I *am* happy. So, please stop. No more matchmaking. I'm super awkward anyway and this makes it way, way worse. So, please. Just stop."

"I met a guy at work yesterday," Katie says.

I close my eyes.

"What work? You work from home," Eliza says.

"Panera work."

"You can't call Panera 'work'. It's not your office."

"Then how come the people at the registers take calls for me sometimes?"

"Girl, you need to do some soul searching."

I laugh.

CHAPTER *Five*

The week goes by in a blur of pouring coffee, scratching down orders, refilling sweet potato fries and attempting to catch a few hours of sleep before my 5am shift every day. Katie and Eliza have transformed the kitchen table into wedding planning central and I feel like everywhere I look, there are magazines, color swatches and appointment cards for cake tasting and venue choices.

What happened to the good old days when it wasn't a huge, expensive thing that required a two-year degree in budgeting and large scale event planning to have a wedding? When my parents got engaged, it took them all of three weeks to plan the wedding and the only reason they waited a couple of months was so they could get married when my dad was on a break from school. They got married in their church and had the reception at Grandma Minnie and Grandpa John's house. They served cake, those little white wedding mints, nuts and some sort of punch.

And that was it.

I've seen the pictures. It was still beautiful. Grandma decorated everything and it was really simple and nice. And I bet the whole thing cost them less than five hundred dollars.

I saw this one statistic when I was flipping through magazines last night while Katie and Eliza were comparing bakeries in town that the average wedding today costs thirty-one *thousand* dollars.

And that doesn't include the cost of a honeymoon.

I mean, if that's not enough to swear you into singlehood forever, I don't know what is.

Thirty-one thousand dollars.

I mean, that's bigger than the down payment I'm saving for on a house.

"Morning, Ash." Katie walks into the kitchen. I'm sitting at the table, rubbing my eyes and trying to find a good spot to set my cereal bowl down that won't mess up invitation samples or fabric swatches.

"Hey."

Katie goes straight for the Keurig and a few seconds later, I hear the now familiar sound of the coffee maker pumping water through the tiny plastic cup.

What happens to all those tiny plastic cups? Instead of teaching or waitressing, I should be focusing all my energy on figuring out how to make sustainable fuel from all the plastic we throw away on an hourly basis.

I could be set for life, if I discovered that.

Maybe then I could afford a thirty-one thousand dollar wedding.

"Finally getting a day off?"

I nod. I have Saturday and Sunday off this week. Two Saturdays off in a row. Weird, because Saturdays are typically nuts at the restaurant and Dad becomes very "all hands on deck". But I guess he could tell that I was starting to drag a little bit.

I'm not nineteen anymore. I can't stay up until one in the morning and be up and ready to go at five like I used to.

I'm not sure how to communicate this to my two best friends.

My devotional time is suffering too. I think I read all of about three words last night before they all started to swim on the page and I had to turn the light out.

I'm still thinking over the "confident access".

The more I think about it, the more I realize that I don't have it.

"That's great!" Katie says, stirring sugar and cream into her coffee. "You can come cake tasting with us!"

I nod. "Sure, that sounds fun," I say because that's what you say. At least I'm not being asked my preference on the exact color of purple Eliza is considering.

Purple is purple.

And it's also the color of a large, child's talking dinosaur show.

I always vote for not purple.

I'm always vetoed, so I don't know why they keep asking me.

76

Katie is still talking. "I think we are going to two bakeries in town and if they both bomb, Eliza was saying maybe drive to St. Louis and try a few there. Then we might stay and get dinner at the Cheesecake Factory. You should come!"

"I can come." Cake tasting can't be too hard, right?

Katie apparently notices that I'm sitting at the table but holding my bowl because there is no place to set anything. "Here, I'll move some of that."

"It's okay."

"So, you liked the linen finish?"

Honestly, I don't remember what I liked. I don't even really remember what dates they've both picked. I think they are both going to be getting married in the fall and all I know is that Eliza was panicking because some wedding book she got off Amazon was saying they should have sent out save the dates three months ago.

"I wasn't even engaged three months ago!" she'd yelled last night. "How am I supposed to follow this timeline if we don't want to be engaged for seven years?"

"Maybe you should just send the invitations since the wedding is already close and then you don't have to pay for postage twice to send both invitations and save the dates?" I'd suggested.

They'd both looked at me like I'd lost my mind.

Maybe there's some sort of vein that runs through the left hand ring finger that supplies oxygen to the brain and when pressure is applied to it that it's not used to, it causes a momentary lapse in judgment that can last the entirety of the engagement period.

I should write out my list for what I want in a wedding right now when there are zero groom possibilities out there so that if I ever get married, I can refer to my list in case the same thing happens to me and all of a sudden I *need* a venue that costs fifteen thousand dollars.

Katie is looking at me like she's waiting for me to answer her about something and I realize she asked me about the invitations. "Oh!" I say. "Right. The linen finish. Sure, I thought it was fine."

"Or, I saw this thing last night where you can make biodegradable cards that have little flower seeds in them and after the wedding, people can plant the invitation and it will grow flowers. Isn't that a cool idea?"

I look at her. "Wait, what?"

"Yeah, so the seeds are like embossed into the card and I don't know how it works, but it seems really neat. And then people have this reminder of your wedding forever."

"Interesting."

"You don't like it?"

"How much are they?"

"Cheaper than the linen finish ones."

"I love them."

Katie grins.

My whole goal in life right now is to keep as much money in my friends' pockets as possible. I know that Katie has been saving for years on the off chance she got married and Eliza has a pretty sizable chunk in a trust account that her mom set up before she died, but there are so many other things they could do with that money than spend it on a gourmet dark chocolate candy bar and hand-lettered invitations.

I mean, it's an event that lasts one night.

A house, on the other hand, can last a lifetime. Or several lifetimes if they invest in something that is built to last.

"You're funny, Ash."

"I'm just trying to help."

"You know, I actually appreciate that about you. But I've been waiting my whole life for this and I don't want to get so sucked in by the finance side of it that it stops being fun."

I nod. "How about I do the finances then and you concentrate on the exciting stuff?"

"Really? Are you really offering that?"

"Sure." If anything, maybe it would help me feel like I'm helping in a way that I can actually help. I'm okay going cake tasting, but really, I don't honestly care that much either way about any of the other decisions they are constantly asking me about. Strapless or sleeves? Don't have an opinion. Venue? Don't have an opinion. Edible invitations or whatever Katie was trying to tell me about?

I really don't care either way.

I think I'm missing a girl gene.

But I'm all over saving money.

"Okay, well, I think Eliza is coming over at ten and then we are going from there," Katie tells me.

I squint at the clock while I crunch my cereal. Eight-thirty. Plenty of time to take a shower and attempt to tame the mane.

"I'd like to go look at dresses tomorrow maybe," Katie says.

I nod. She's been a few times. Eliza and I both went with her once and I know Katie and Eliza went at least twice. Katie still can't find one she wants. Eliza found a dress the first place we went to.

Katie looked stunning in every single dress she tried on so I'm not sure why she didn't end up with any of them, but I didn't press the matter. I think she has this idea in her head and until she finds the one that fits that idea, it's not going to work.

She's like that with everything else, so I guess it shouldn't shock me that she's like that with her wedding.

It's a good thing that Luke is so laid back.

Though I guess it's hard to be uptight in a cardigan.

I think her mentioning this is Katie's way of asking me to go though, so I nod again. "I'll go with you, if you want."

"Really? Oh thanks, Ash! I hate going wedding dress shopping alone."

Katie's mom doesn't live in town but her grandmother does. "Have you asked your grandmother to go with you?" I ask her.

"Gram hates shopping," Katie says.

"I bet she wouldn't hate shopping for your wedding dress," I tell her.

"Yeah, but she would comment on the prices and the styles and…" Katie shrugs. "I don't know. I want her to come but I want her to want to come."

I look at Katie and I know she really does want her grandmother there.

Maybe this is why she hasn't actually bought one yet.

"Have you actually asked her?" I ask again.

"I mean, I've mentioned it," Katie says.

"Like mentioned it how? In typical Katie way or in regular person way?"

Katie rolls her eyes. "I asked her!"

"You said, 'Gram, will you go wedding dress shopping with me?'"

"No, I said, 'Gram, I'm going to look at dresses on Saturday.'"

I shake my head and half-laugh. "So you didn't ask her."

"I implied! I very heavily implied. And I even did the eyebrow thing and she still didn't say she wanted to come."

"What eyebrow thing?"

"You know. This thing." She tips her head and sort of raises both eyebrows in a *soo?* look that Katie has perfected.

"Oh good grief. Call your grandmother."

"Ash."

"No 'Ash'. Call her."

"Ash, I'm fine."

I stand up, pick up the chair I'm sitting on, carry it to the front door, set it directly in front of the door and plop down.

"I'm not moving from this chair until you call your grandmother."

"Oh, for Pete's sake."

"Guess you'll be late to eat cake."

"I can go out the garage door, Ash."

"But you won't leave me sitting here. You're too nice."

Katie looks at me, mouth in a straight line. "Fine."

"Fine."

She picks up her phone off the kitchen counter and pushes a couple of buttons on the screen, holding it to her ear.

I can hear her Gram's voice answer, which to me says that either Katie is deaf or she needs to turn her phone volume down or both.

"Hi Gram," Katie says. "It's me. Yes, hi. So, I'm thinking about going wedding dress shopping tomorrow afternoon."

She stops and looks at me and I make that motion with my hands that people do in charades to tell people to keep talking.

She rolls her eyes but finishes the thought. "And I was wondering if you wanted to come with me."

I can hear Gram's squeal and Katie immediately gasps and pulls the phone away from her ear.

Maybe that will teach her to turn down the volume. Sheesh. She's going to become a subject in one of those Buzz Feed articles about how constant cell phone use has caused this entire generation to become hard of hearing at a ridiculously young age.

Katie arranges to pick up her grandmother at two o'clock and then hangs up.

I look at her, still in my chair. "See? I told you so."

"You know, one of the things I appreciate the most about our friendship is how you never rub my nose in it when you're right and I'm wrong. I really treasure that about us."

"Mm-hmm. You can thank me later."

She throws a dish towel from the kitchen counter at me and then stalks down the hall. "We are going to be ready to leave in an hour!" she yells over her shoulder.

"Yes, master."

Her door closes and I grin.

Exactly an hour later, I am filling up my water bottle with water from the fridge. I'm dressed in a black sleeveless sundress, my hair is out of control curly thanks to this humidity and I have on my sandals.

Basically, this is as good as I get. In about ten minutes, my hair is going to get the kibosh and I'm going to pull it up in the elastic band that I always have with me.

Katie comes into the kitchen and she looks beautiful because she's Katie and she always does.

"Cute dress," she nods to me.

"Thanks!" I tighten the lid on my water bottle. "It has pockets."

"I can see that."

"I like pockets."

"You are such a nerd."

"You don't like pockets?"

She ignores me and grabs two bottled Frappucino things from the fridge. Katie and Eliza drink coffee like it's water.

If I drank that much caffeine on a regular basis, I would never sleep again.

Though, maybe I could use all those extra awake hours to figure out the whole plastic into fuel thing.

Eliza opens the front door. "My car or your car?" she asks Katie.

"Mine. More seats."

"There's only three of us," I say, going through the laundry room into the garage. "It's not like we need a bus or anything."

Katie opens the garage door and Eliza and Mike are both standing in the driveway.

"Hi." I go around to the back of Katie's little crossover SUV and open the back door so I can climb in.

I'm not sure why Mike is here but maybe he's seeing us off or something weird like that. Actually, it wouldn't shock me if he were. He's pretty overprotective about Eliza.

"Wait, Ash, I need to fix the backseat," Katie says to me.

I look in the car and it's spotless. "There's nothing back here."

"No, I know, but I need to raise the third row."

"A modern-day miracle. This is why I've nicknamed your third row 'Lazarus'," Eliza says.

Katie laughs and reaches around me, pulling a little handle and up pops a bench seat from the depths of the cargo area.

"I told Luke we were leaving at nine-thirty, so he should be here in a couple of minutes," Katie says, looking at her watch.

It's almost ten.

Luke is the most tardy person I have ever met in my life. And it's like he has no concept of this. I have no idea how he has been so successful as a wedding singer. I mean, aren't those gigs kind of time sensitive? He works from home the rest of the time doing IT stuff, so I guess he doesn't need to be on time for anything in that job, but still.

I know it makes Katie nuts but it looks like she's figured out a way around it.

"So, um, Luke is coming," I say, in a quiet voice so the other two can't hear me.

"Right."

"And Mike."

Katie nods. "Yes."

"I can probably assume that Cooper is going to be joining us as well then, right?"

Katie grins. "Not just another pretty face, are you?"

I let my breath out and it sounds very close to a growl.

"What?"

"Y'all are trying to set me up with Mike," I hiss because even though I'm mad, I'm still polite about it.

Katie shakes her head. "I swear, Ash, I am not trying to set you up. Eliza said he was interested in coming."

"Eliza has made it no secret that she wants Mike and I to end up together."

"Well, I can't speak for Eliza, but I promise, I am not trying to set the two of you up. I don't set anyone up. Good grief, I can barely get Jell-O to set up."

I smirk. Katie grins. "Just settle down, Ash. I'm sure it's nothing."

"It's awkward."

"It's only awkward if you make it awkward."

I hate this saying with every fiber of my being. It makes no sense at all. Does this mean that I am in control of other people's feelings too? Does this mean by me acting all cool and collected that other people will too? If so, I have way more influence than I ever imagined.

But I don't. It's all a ridiculous saying that someone came up with to make other people feel better.

Probably someone like Eliza who was setting someone like me up on a blind date with Mr. Personality.

I take a deep breath and blow it through my pursed lips.

Katie grins. "There you go. Fight the anger with yoga breathing."

"Who's angry?" Eliza is suddenly behind me and she takes one look at my face and grins. "Ah."

"Come on, Eliza."

"What? He asked what I was doing today and I told him and he asked if he could tag along. I couldn't say no, he's my brother and the only family I have left in the *entire* world."

Eliza is skilled in a lot of things. She's an amazing nurse, she's a great cook, she is an excellent home decorator.

That being said, she is possibly the worst when it comes to tact or trying to cover something up. She's totally stretching the truth here and I know it. I would bet you my next paycheck from Minnie's that she called him, not the other way around.

Katie obviously thinks the same thing I do because we both look at her with a "how dumb do you think we are" expression and Eliza grins all toothily at us before calling shotgun and hopping in the front seat.

Swell.

Luke pulls up in front of the house right then and climbs out of his car, tucking his keys in his pocket as he ambles up the driveway. Luke is nothing if not relaxed.

"Hey guys," he says, grinning his trademark smile at everyone and leaning down to kiss Katie's cheek, who immediately blushes like she's thirteen.

It's pretty much the most adorable thing I've seen all week.

"Hi," Katie grins and they stand there holding hands and looking all lovestruck at each other.

For a long time, I was worried that Katie had been waiting for Mr. Right for so long that she wouldn't even recognize him when she showed up. She dated one or two people right before she met Luke who seemed like decent people but I guess there was no chemistry.

It's obvious to everyone in a twelve-block radius that there's chemistry with Luke.

I accept the inevitable and lift the hatch on Katie's car and climb in the very back seat so Luke and Mike can sit in the middle. I'm the shortest by quite a bit and I can't really imagine the men being able to climb in back here.

But really, I should have gone with my jeans. Pockets or not, this dress was not made for climbing.

Crossover SUVs get great gas mileage but they really aren't the best choice for transporting too many more than four people around.

Mike climbs in behind Eliza, Luke is behind Katie and we are off. The girls chat happily with Luke about cake and tasting etiquette.

"Wait, so you don't get a whole slice to eat?"

"Oh goodness, no," Eliza says. "I think you'll probably get like a one inch square."

"That's it?"

"Well, I mean, you'll probably get a few different flavors."

"And we're going to at least two different shops," Katie says. "You'll probably get the equivalent of a few slices."

"That's a lot of sugar," Mike says.

Eliza sighs.

I think I remember her mentioning that Mike was a bit of a health nut.

Luke grins over at Mike. "I have a feeling that these girls don't care too much about the sugar intake," he says. "I mean, I've been around when they might as well have been spooning the sugar out of the bowl straight into their mouths."

Eliza is shaking her head at Luke and he grins, unrepentant.

Mike is obviously clamping his mouth shut.

Well, kudos to him for not taking the bait.

"They've done studies that sugar is worse for the human brain than heroin," Mike says.

And maybe not.

This is not the best conversation to be having right before we spend the day trying out a bunch of different cakes.

Luke is still smiling because he's Luke and I've never seen him actually mad about anything. "Don't worry, Mike. I'll get Katie into some sort of therapy right after the honeymoon."

Katie and Eliza start laughing and it totally breaks the tension Mike brought in here.

Bless Luke.

Katie found a keeper.

We get to the first bakery and Katie parks and we all climb out. I feel a little bit like we are a bunch of clowns exiting a clown car.

I should have driven myself.

Cooper is standing right inside the door, eyes closed.

Eliza pokes him. "Are you still alive?"

"Shh. I'm having a moment with the smells in here."

Eliza rolls her eyes. "You're weird."

"Some would argue that since you've chosen to marry me of your own volition, that would make you weirder." Cooper opens his eyes and grins at his fiancée.

"Hi."

"Hi."

I look away, feeling very out of place. I should've let Katie and Eliza come with the boys. All cake is good. It's not like they really need my opinion here.

But since I didn't drive myself, I'm now stuck for the rest of the day.

Based on the way Mike is standing all straight backed, hands in pockets and stoic-faced, I'm assuming he feels like he doesn't belong either.

Too bad he isn't friendlier. We could be talking.

Part of me wants to try and engage him in a conversation but I don't even know where to start. Every time I've ever talked to him, he's been pretty closed off. So, I don't even know if we have anything in common to talk about.

Apparently, sugar consumption is not a good thing to discuss.

Better not mention my family's business. Minnie has built a living on people coming back for her pies. And I've seen those pies being made and let's just say they are not anywhere close to sugar free.

"Hello, can I help you?" A girl close to our age wearing an apron and her hair in a low, short ponytail appears behind a display case full of cakes, cupcakes and chocolate-covered delicacies.

I suddenly realize that she works in a place that smells like heaven every day.

I should have been a baker.

My parents would argue that I had every chance of that and I turned it down to go sit in a classroom with a bunch of germy children.

These are the same people who keep pressuring me to get married and have germy children of my own.

Katie tells the girl we are here for a cake tasting and she nods. "Come on back to our cake tasting room," the girl says.

We follow her around the counter to a tiny little back room where they have somehow managed to fit eight chairs and a little coffee table. The paint is a deep gray and there's lamps everywhere and a tiny, tiny window. A few little pallet wood signs with cutesy sayings about cake and coffee are on the walls.

It's cute, if not a little claustrophobic.

"My name is Stephanie," the girl says. "Can I get you guys anything to drink? We have water, tea, coffee…"

"Coffee," both Katie and Eliza immediately say.

"Same for me," Cooper nods.

"Eh, why not?" Luke says.

"What kind of tea do you have?" Mike asks.

"I have black or green. Both hot tea."

"I'll have green."

She looks at me. "And for you?"

"Just water, please."

"I'll be right back. Please make yourselves comfortable."

We all sit down as best we can. The guys' knees are all mashed up against the coffee table and Katie and Eliza are oo-ing over the signs on the wall.

"Oh, that one is so cute!" Eliza says, pointing to one of the ones about cake.

"I should add on a room like this to my house," Katie says. "We could make it the cake room. What do you think, Ash?"

I smile. "That could work."

Katie is so sweet. She's never once mentioned me getting the boot since she's getting married and she's never once made me feel uncomfortable about still living with her. I really appreciate that about her. But I can read the writing on the wall.

"Okay." Stephanie is back with a tray filled with drinks and the cutest little tiny cakes I've ever seen.

She hands out the cups and starts passing around tiny clear plastic plates and little forks.

"So, I have three different cakes for you to sample," she says. "And if you are hoping for something different, you can definitely let me know and I'll do my best to accommodate you. These are our three most popular wedding cake choices."

I take the plate and there are three little cakes that almost look like petite fours on it. They are all covered in smooth white icing and they each have one tiny icing flower on the top of them in different colors.

"Okay, so our first cake is a lemon poppy seed with blueberry filling and a white buttercream frosting," she says. "It's going to be the cake with the yellow flower on top."

I hate poppy seed and so I do my best to choke it down quickly so I don't seem to be rude. The others are going on and on about how delicious it is. Mike takes a tiny bite and then a long swig of his green tea.

I've tried green tea before. I had the flu and one of my cousins, Marsha, convinced me it might help me get better faster.

I should have called Marsha to come help me scrub green tea out of my carpet when I drank it and threw it all right back up before I could even make it to the bathroom.

Needless to say, green tea and I aren't on the best of terms anymore.

Blegh. But it might get the taste of poppy seeds out of my mouth.

I do my best to casually drink some water and Stephanie points to the cake with the pink rose on top. "The next cake is a almond amaretto cake with a rich vanilla bean custard filling and a white chocolate buttercream frosting."

I think in certain circles, people have refined their palates enough to actually be able to taste all these

95

individual flavors. I don't know if it's the years of drinking sodas or not, but for the life of me, it just tastes like cake.

Katie and Eliza, though, are raving.

Raving.

"Oh. My. Gosh," Eliza says and I have to physically bite my tongue to not burst out into a Janice impression and start yelling, "CHANDLER BING!"

Not the time or place, Ashten. Not the time or place.

"Holy cow, this is the best cake I have *ever* had. And I've had a lot of cake," Katie declares.

Stephanie nods, obviously pleased. "Wonderful, wonderful!"

The boys obviously are fans because their mouths are full and they all are giving thumbs up.

"And our last cake," Stephanie says, "Is what we call our 'Black Heart' cake."

Doesn't seem like the best name for a wedding cake, but then again, what do I know? Plus, maybe it's named for someone in particular. A groom, perhaps. Or, perhaps a mother of the bride.

I've heard they can be horrible.

Though, I know both Katie and Eliza would give their right arms for their mothers to be here planning this with them. Katie's lives too far away and is apparently ridiculously busy with Katie's much younger twin siblings and Eliza's mom passed away a few years ago.

I think Eliza stuffed it down and didn't deal with it until recently, so it's so good to see her grieving and realizing that she can still risk people getting close.

"This cake is a dark chocolate and salted caramel swirled cake with a rich chocolate ganache and raspberry filling and a white buttercream frosting to keep it nice and light for the wedding day."

Nothing about this cake is nice and light. It's delicious, but it's so rich, it's like eating a piece of fudge covered in frosting.

I can only handle about a centimeter before I start to worry that my teeth are going to decay in front of me, all *Pirates of the Caribbean* style.

The girls and Luke have no trouble eating theirs. But I notice that Cooper only eats half of his and Mike doesn't look like he ate any of his.

"Wow," Eliza says, sitting back in her chair and downing her coffee. "That was amazing."

"Incredible," Katie nods. "Thank you so much, Stephanie."

"Of course. I know you'd mentioned that we are your first stop, so if you would like to go ahead and order, let me know, otherwise I will look forward to your call."

Confidence. You have to appreciate that in a baker.

"Thanks. We will."

We all gather our stuff and walk out and God bless him, Cooper takes one look at Katie's car and says, "Yeah, I'll drive separately." So, Eliza decides to ride with him and I am officially spared from climbing back into the third row back seat.

"So that last cake," Mike says, climbing in behind Luke, who is now driving.

Katie is in the passenger seat and I'm clicking my seatbelt in the seat behind her. Its very awkward to be in this tiny car right by Mike but I am trying my best not to think of it.

Especially since Mike was basically locked out of Cooper's car and forced to ride with us.

He does not look happy about it.

Well, neither am I.

"It was amazing, wasn't it?" Katie is still licking her lips.

"It was really rich," I say.

"It was very rich. I think my favorite was the second one. All those intricate flavors! What did you think, honey?"

Luke is sitting with his right arm stretched across the back of Katie's seat and he's lightly playing with a lock of her perfect hair. "Honestly, I liked them all," he says.

I figured.

Luke is possibly the least picky person I've ever met. I feel like Stephanie could have sat us down and given us a cake make out of soggy Goldfish crackers all squished together and he would have found something good about it.

He would have been all, "Look at the beautiful yellow color! I love yellow cakes!"

I really need to stop giving Luke such a hard time.

Even if it is in my head. Poor guy is a good man and has been great for Katie. He's really good to her. They're one of those couples who I bet will be married for fifty years and never fight once.

They're both too nice.

Nice people should only marry each other. Otherwise, one always gets walked all over in the marriage and it's no good for anyone.

I mean, look at Jane and Mr. Bingley in *Pride and Prejudice*. If Jane had married Mr. Darcy, it would have been horrible and they would have ended up living in separate wings of Pemberley for the rest of forever.

It would be all *Beauty and the Beast* only without the talking chandelier.

Or lampstand.

Really, what was Lumiere? A menorah?

Anyway.

Luke is still talking. "So, really, I thought they were all really fantastic. I'd be fine with any of those."

Katie is not sure. "Even the first one?"

"Even the first one. Loved it."

"Ash, what did you think of how they tasted?"

Great.

I quickly think of adjectives that don't necessarily have to convey my like or dislike of anything I had today. "I thought they were all beautiful," I say. And they were.

It's sort of like complimenting someone's hair when they ask what you think of their dress, though.

Katie turns in her seat and narrows her eyes at me. "I did not ask if you liked how they looked. I asked if you liked how they tasted."

"They were all very moist."

Though, the last one was moist and dense.

Apologies to anyone out there who hates that word.

Katie is apparently one of those people. "Really, Ash?" she makes a face and turns back around in her seat, shuddering. "You couldn't find a different word?"

"They all appeared to be somewhere between soggy and dry."

Luke looks back at me in the rear view mirror, laughing. "Nice, Ashten."

Even Mike cracks a half-smile.

Part of me is very pleased with this. Though, I guess even the Grinch was known to smile occasionally.

CHAPTER *Six*

By six o'clock Saturday night, I am so full of cake, I am starting to Google how to tell if you have been a victim of cake overdose. I am pretty sure this is how gluten intolerances begin. No wonder people typically gain weight after they get married.

It's all the cake tasting come back for their waistlines.

We have been to five bakeries and it doesn't feel like Katie and Eliza are any closer to a decision. After the fourth bakery, I could honestly not remember what any of the previous cake choices were. I'm pretty sure that at the end of the day, they all tasted exactly the same.

And now, I'm not even sure I like cake anymore. I am one hundred percent in favor of them scrapping the cake idea and doing like an ice cream bar or a s'more roast or something that doesn't involve anything resembling a sweet bread-like substance surrounded by what is basically sweetened sugar.

And dear goodness, I need to get away from Mike because I am starting to sound just like him.

At this last bakery, he refused to even taste anything.

"So, how about we call it a night and go get dinner?" Cooper says as we all prepare to get back into our cars.

We've been in St. Louis since about two o'clock this afternoon and so I'm also already calculating how long until we are back home.

It's about an hour and a half drive if there's no traffic.

I know of people who live in Carrington Springs and commute to St. Louis for work and I think they have to have lost their minds. Three hours in traffic minimum every single day is not worth whatever small town feel Carrington Springs gives you or your children.

Plus, I figure the children would rather see their parents for those three hours than live somewhere like Carrington Springs anyway.

Cooper lives here still, so he's not looking at a long drive home.

However, since he lives here, I imagine I'll be kicked to the third row again for the drive back.

Ugh.

Really, dresses should all come with an option to sort of zip up the middle just in case you find yourself having to climb into the backseat of a small SUV while wearing one. Yes, you'd look like a throwback from the 80s, but at least you wouldn't be at risk of flashing everyone in a two mile radius.

At least it will be dark going home. A few less people in the flash zone.

"Dinner sounds great!" Eliza is bubbling and I can't decide if it's the sugar intake or the fact that she's spent an entire day with her fiancé. Eliza and Cooper rarely get to see each other and the days they do, she always comes home bouncing like Tigger on an energy drink high.

It's actually kind of cute.

"What sounds good?" Luke asks, flipping Katie's keys around his index finger. Luke basically commandeered Katie's car and he's hasn't stopped driving.

I love Luke but I will never be a passenger in a car he is driving again after today. He's too laid back. We almost got hit like forty-two times.

Needless to say, I've repented of all my sins and I'm ready to go should the way home end badly.

"I think the original thought was the Cheesecake Factory, but honestly, guys, I don't know if I can do more dessert," Cooper says.

Everyone nods and it's the first time in my life I've ever seen Katie or Eliza turn down dessert.

Apparently I'm not the only one a little green right now.

"There's a good salad buffet on the way back out of town," Mike suggests.

"That actually sounds great," Katie says. "I think we might need to eat plain kale to counteract the rest of the day's calories."

We pile back into the two cars and it takes about fifteen minutes to get to the restaurant. Mostly because we miss three green lights because someone is never in any kind of a rush to get anywhere and is driving five miles an hour under the speed limit.

I would die if I had to ride with Luke every day.

Based on Mike's hands clasped together and how white his knuckles are, I'm assuming he's feeling the same way.

I will always and forevermore either stay home or take my own car.

The salad buffet is pretty busy, which I always look for in a restaurant. If anything, growing up at Minnie's has taught me that if there isn't consistently a wait somewhere, it's probably not worth going to.

There are about ten people in the line ahead of us, already filling their plates along the buffet line and Luke passes out trays to everyone.

I take my dark green tray and wait behind the couples. Cooper and Eliza are first, Luke and Katie are next. Mike and I are standing there all awkwardly.

Just stay home. This will become my new mantra for life.

Want to go cake tasting, Ashten?

No, thank you. I am going to stay home.

Want to come with us to get ice cream?

No, thanks. I'm going to stay home. Mostly because of the way Eliza keeps grinning at Mike and me. It's not helping the awkwardness.

Mike kind of does this weird gesture with his hand for me to go first and I nod, stepping slightly in front of him. "Thanks."

"Sure."

The other two couples are happily chatting, Eliza is grinning at Cooper, eyes shining, Luke and Katie are snuggling together while they load their plates full of lettuce. I've never seen people snuggle in a salad bar line.

It's a little sickening, actually.

"I agree."

I look back at Mike. "I'm sorry?"

He nods to the others. "It's nauseating."

And apparently he can read my mind. But I have to pretend that I'm happy for my friends, not disgusted by them. "What are you talking about?" I ask, trying to come across as super supportive of everything they do.

"I saw you shake your head. It's weird. And it's even weirder for me, because Cooper has been my best friend forever."

I hadn't considered that. "I forgot that you guys have been friends for so long."

"He's basically my brother. It's a little bit of an 'I'm My Own Grandpa' thing for me with my brother marrying my sister."

I smile.

What do you know. Mike made a joke.

Maybe all that sugar was good for him too. It seems to have made him a little sweeter.

Grandma Minnie used to say that about her pies. I can remember being tiny and standing next to her at the carryout window before the restaurant expanded again and her handing a customer a pie and telling them, "Thank you for your purchase! We know this will make your friends and family a little sweeter."

Mike immediately clears his throat and looks away and maybe I was a little preemptive with my thoughts on the sweetness.

I load my plate with spinach and romaine lettuce and go down the line, adding shredded carrots, cucumbers, bell peppers and sunflower seeds.

Mike bypasses the dressing. "Did you know that most salads have more calories than a hamburger because of the dressings that people put on them?"

I have seriously just put raspberry vinaigrette all over my salad.

"That's encouraging," I say.

"It's something to be aware of. Besides, most dressings that aren't homemade or organic are full of artificial ingredients, sweeteners and food dyes."

"So the alternative is undressed vegetables?"

"I'm about to ask for plain balsamic vinegar."

Once a week, Grandma Minnie reduces down a huge pot of balsamic vinegar to make the glaze for her legendary pork chops. The smell is so strong that she has to declare the kitchen in a state of balsamic emergency and she only does it when the restaurant is closed and all the employees have gone home. It's one of those smells that you can't get away from and every Thursday, I swear the restaurant still smells all acidic, even if it's not the eye-watering cloud that it is on Wednesday night.

Grandma Minnie though sits over the pot and breathes it in. She says it's good for your lungs.

I think she's smelled it too much and now it's affected her brain.

"Excuse me," Mike says to the guy behind the counter who is likely about sixteen. He's got acne and braces and no one ever taught the poor child to stand up straight, so he has this schlumpy appearance that looks even worse with his apron and hat.

He looks at Mike and finally, Mike continues since it's apparent that the boy cannot speak. "Do you have balsamic vinegar?"

The kid points to the dressing table where a vat of balsamic vinaigrette is sunken into the counter. "Yup."

"No, I mean, *plain* balsamic vinegar."

The others have already paid for their meals and are sitting at the table, obviously waiting for us to come so they can pray.

"Don't think so," the kid says.

Mike's mouth is a hard line now as he looks at the boy, who yes, needs to be more customer-oriented, but still.

"Um, I'm done," I say meekly, showing him my plate.

"Do you want a drink?"

"Yes please."

"Are you together?"

Mike does this sort of snort-chuckle thing.

I am going to kill Eliza.

"No," I say, quietly.

"Twelve dollars, sixteen cents."

I hand the boy my credit card, take my receipt and go sit down at the table next to Katie. They've segregated the girls to one side of the table and the boys to the other, which means I now get to look at Mike for the entire rest of the meal.

I mean, he's just rude.

I do not see how Eliza is so normal and Mike is so not. And for that matter, Eliza didn't have a choice in who her brother is, but Cooper totally has a choice in who his friends are. Why is he even friends with Mike? Cooper seems so kind and generous and funny and Mike is awful. They have absolutely nothing in common. Cooper would have probably made a joke if the restaurant guy had asked me and Cooper that question. Not snorted and been all *as if* like Cher on *Clueless.*

So I'm not as pretty as Katie or as thin as Eliza. You don't have to be all mean about it.

Mike sits down opposite me with his plain pile of vegetables and there's a small part deep in my chest is happy they didn't have any vinegar for him.

He deserves untasty vegetables.

"Let me pray," Cooper says from his spot across from Eliza. "Jesus, we thank You for this food, we thank You for this company, we praise You for these good friends."

Not all of them, Lord. Not all of them.

I peek across the table and then squinch my eyes closed again.

Sorry, Lord. Except I'm not sorry.

"Bless the food to our bodies and help it to counteract all the cake we consumed earlier today. Amen."

The girls and Luke start smiling and chuckling. Mike just kind of shakes his head.

Grinch.

Seriously, how is Cooper friends with Mike? And how have they been friends for so long? Did Mike used to be nicer or something?

I shove my salad in my mouth as fast I as I can, hoping that maybe the others will follow suit and we can leave here sooner rather than later.

It doesn't work. The girls are picking at their food, chatting about cakes and which one was their favorite and how they loved the icing at the third bakery but hated the cake and loved the cake at the first bakery, but didn't necessarily love the decoration.

"I mean, maybe the taste should outweigh the look," Eliza says. "I remember what the cakes taste like at weddings I've been to instead of what they looked like."

"Yeah, but it will be in all of your pictures forever," Katie says. "And most people won't always remember what the cake tasted like."

"Cooper will," Eliza says.

"I will," Cooper nods. "I remember almost everything about food."

Katie laughs. "Like seriously?"

"Seriously. I am a food-savant. Ask me what I had for breakfast at any given point in time and I can tell you."

"May 14th, 2002," Luke says.

"Peanut butter toast, a banana and a bowl of oatmeal," Cooper rattles off.

"Impressive," Luke says, "Though, I have no way to correlate it with the truth, so as far as I know, good job."

Eliza rolls her eyes. "Don't listen to him. He knows that because he has had the same thing for breakfast every single day of his entire life."

"You need to get out more," Katie tells him.

"I need to introduce you to Christmas eggs," Luke says.

"What are Christmas eggs?"

"My mom's specialty," Luke tells him. "Onion, green bell pepper, red bell pepper. You sauté them all in a little bit of butter and then add in some scrambled eggs and cook until the eggs are done. It's amazing. Best way to wake up."

Katie makes a face and shudders. "I do not do eggs in the morning."

Mike frowns at her. "When do you do them?"

"I like them when I'm having breakfast for dinner. Just cannot handle them before about ten in the morning. I don't even like the smell of them until after lunch."

"Guess your Christmas egg days are over," Mike says to Luke.

"Bummer because I got a new egg maker machine thing," Luke says.

I look at him. "Isn't that called a skillet?"

"It used to be called a skillet. Then my mom bought me this little deal for my birthday. It cooks the eggs and the

111

pepper mixture separately and then drops them together right before it's served. It's called like the Good Cooker, or something like that."

"Oh!" Eliza bursts. "The Eggs-cellent Extra! I've seen those on TV!"

"Surely it is not really called that," I protest.

"Yep, that's it," Luke says. "The Eggs-cellent Extra. One purpose and it takes up a whole cabinet in the kitchen."

"Which means it's getting the boot when we get married," Katie says. "We don't have the cabinet space for appliances to take up an entire cabinet for only one function."

"I could keep it in the garage and cook my eggs in there," Luke says.

"Then you could share your eggs with the mice you'll attract," Eliza says to him.

"Exactly."

"Eggs-actly," Cooper corrects.

Even Mike laughs.

I settle down in bed a few hours later and pull over my Bible.

I cannot stop thinking about the "confident access".

Lord, I don't think I have the confidence thing down.

I mean, one snort from Mike and my self-esteem has completely plummeted.

And I don't even like Mike.

I try to think of some of the most confident people I know and I immediately can think of one right away – my Grandma Minnie.

She is hands down the wisest, most confident in who she is person I have ever met.

And she knows more Scripture than anyone I've ever heard of. She can rattle off verses at the drop of a hat. You come in complaining about something and she has a verse for it.

One time, I came into the restaurant with the worst headache ever and Grandma Minnie put both her hands on my shoulders and started praying, "Lord, You said in Psalm 30 that if we cry out to You for help, You will heal and Jesus, we cry to You to heal my sweet Ashten from this headache. And if not, Lord, give her the strength to carry on."

And then she hugged me tight and told me, "All right then, dear one, we've given it to Jesus." And she sent me on my way, totally believing that God would take care of it.

I want to be like her so badly.

CHAPTER *Seven*

I'm just sitting down to a quick breakfast before church the next morning when Katie walks in, sliding her earrings through her ear lobes and nodding to me. "Morning, Ash. You feeling better?"

I don't remember feeling bad, so I'm not sure how to answer the question. "Better than what?" I ask.

"You seemed down last night. I figured maybe the cake wasn't sitting well. Goodness knows it messed my stomach up. I can't even remember the last time I had cake, much less that much in one day." She rubs her nonexistent stomach and sighs. "I'm not even going to eat sugar for the next few months to prepare myself."

As she's talking, she's brewing a cup of coffee in the Keurig and then pouring cream and spooning sugar into the cup.

I almost say something.

But then I remember I'm not Mike.

Oops. Sorry Lord.

Last night, after I closed my Bible, I laid there for like twenty minutes, staring at the ceiling and continuing to hear his little snort when the waiter guy asked if we were together.

I don't know why it's bugging me so much but it is. It's not like I *like* Mike. And I honestly do not even care what he thinks. But I don't know. Maybe the sting never goes away.

Rejection is never fun, regardless of who it is from. Plus, then it brought up all these bad memories of Daniel.

When he'd told me he'd gotten a job offer for Alaska, I remember thinking, *well, surely he will turn it down because of us*. Especially since the entire time we dated, he kept saying things like, "I have this great feeling about us" or "I'm so excited that we are together" or my personal favorite now, looking back, "I really think God arranged everything to have us end up together."

Or not.

That was before the Dream Job in Alaska called. So maybe God arranged everything for him to move there instead.

But you know. Semantics.

Whatever the reason, we obviously were not supposed to end up together.

A saying I hate, by the way. You don't "end up" with your spouse. If anything, I've noticed with Katie and Eliza that it can take a lot of work for people to get married.

I mean the cake consumption alone is enough to kill some people.

Anyway. I spent a good part before falling asleep praying that if God can't give me confidence, to at least give me tolerance with Mike. And I kept being reminded of that verse in Galatians where Paul tells them to do good to all people, especially those who love Christ.

Mike is a Christian, so I guess he ranks in the "especially" category.

Katie is looking at me like she's waiting for me to say something, but I'm not sure what I'm supposed to say. "I'm fine," I say.

She gives me one of her patented looks over her coffee mug and I know she isn't convinced.

The front door opens and Eliza sticks her head in right as Katie opens her mouth. "Shotgun!" Eliza yells.

"No, no, no!" I say to her. "I had to ride in the back the entire day yesterday! The very back! In a *dress*."

"It's true," Katie says, sipping her coffee. "It was a cute dress, though. You looked adorable. You always look adorable, but you looked especially adorable yesterday."

So adorable I made someone snort at the thought of being with me.

Simmer down, girl.

Eliza comes all the way in the house and she's halfway dressed.

At least she has on pants under her robe.

There have been a few times where she's walked across the street and if my Grandma Minnie would have seen her, the lectures would be swift and loud.

Young ladies do not pretend that tights are pants.

Grandma Minnie isn't the world's biggest fan of leggings.

"I didn't like them the first time around and I don't like them now," she always tells me.

Eliza is a bit more of a free spirit when it comes to these things. I'm curious how marriage is going to change her. Or if it will.

"You do realize we are leaving here in five minutes," Katie says to her, looking at the clock on the microwave.

"Yes. I realize that. I have to work tonight too."

"Night shift?"

"Yeah."

"Bummer." Katie pulls a granola bar out of the pantry and opens it. "That is a robe, right? Not some weird shirt of yours?"

And apparently Katie shares my opinion on Eliza and her particular style of clothing.

Eliza rolls her eyes. "Y'all have no appreciation for style."

"I like knowing that my shirts are shirts."

"To each his own," Eliza says. "But yes, this is my robe. Can I borrow that purple-y top you wore last week with that gray flowered skirt thing?"

Katie frowns. "What purple top?"

"It's like a fake wrap looking one?"

"Oh yeah. Um. Sure."

"I don't have to borrow it. I was just wondering. But if you don't want me to, I won't."

"No, it's fine. But I want it back."

Eliza sighs. "One time!"

I smirk. Apparently, one time Katie went over to Eliza's house to borrow a jacket and found one of her own shirts in Eliza's closet, all washed and hung up.

"It's in my closet."

"Thank you." Eliza disappears.

"Thank you for never borrowing my clothes," Katie says to me.

"Please. I can't wear your clothes."

Katie rolls her eyes. "Let's not even get started down that gravy train."

"What is a gravy train?"

"I have no idea but Gram tells me that all the time."

I grin. I love Katie's Gram.

Eliza reappears, holding her robe and wearing Katie's shirt, which I would have called more of a grayish-blue than

118

a purple. Maybe that's why Katie didn't know what she was talking about at first.

"Does this look okay?"

The shirt is one of those wrap-styles that accentuates her tiny ribcage. She's wearing cuffed skinny jeans and Sperrys.

"Looks great," Katie nods.

"Very nice," I say, finishing up my breakfast. When Katie says we are leaving in five minutes, she means that she is backing out of the garage in five minutes, whether we are in the car or not. Katie is nothing if not punctual.

I feel like she might kill Luke one of these days when the rosy glow of newlywed joy wears off because I've never known him to be anything but at least twenty minutes late to everything.

She'll probably even write it on his headstone:

Luke Brantley. Beloved Husband and Father.
I said five minutes.

I grab my purse and Bible and head to the garage to claim my shotgun spot.

Instead, I find Eliza climbing into the passenger seat.

"Hey!" I say.

She grins. "Sorry. I forgot. Wait, I called it! By the rules of the shotgun, I should get to sit here." She slides her left foot back into the car.

"No ma'am. Not today. I am done sitting in the back."

"I get car sick."

"You do not."

"My legs are longer than yours and so I need the legroom."

"You are barely two inches taller than me!"

"I have recurrent nightmares because one time, I got left in the backseat of a car and it had the child lock function on and I couldn't get the door open and it took my old college roommate like twelve minutes before she stopped talking long enough to realize that I wasn't even around to be listening to her story."

I look at her. "You couldn't just climb through to the front seat?"

"I was in a skirt!"

I look at her and shake my head. "Okay, fine, sit in the front."

She grins and plops down in the seat. "You're the best, Ash!"

"Yeah, yeah."

I close her door and open the back door.

Katie comes out of the house, makes sure we are both in the garage, then opens the garage door and climbs into

120

HAPPILY EVER Ashton

the car, sliding her glasses onto her face. She tips them down her nose, though, and looks at me in the rearview mirror.

"Girl, you need to be meaner."

"Thanks for the life advice there, Katie. I'm practicing Galatians."

Eliza grins. "My arthritis is acting up. We will probably get rain today."

"Didn't make it to that excuse?" I ask, rolling my eyes.

"I thought it was a good one. I can feel it in my knees."

"Please. You are barely thirty years old. You cannot feel rain in your knees."

"I could if I wanted to."

"She is one with nature," Katie says to me in the rearview mirror. "Didn't you know this?"

I grin. Eliza might be possibly the most anti-nature girl I've ever met, next to myself. I'm pretty certain that one time, Eliza killed a plastic plant.

That takes a special kind of talent.

Not to mention the fact that any time I've seen her outside, Eliza complains the whole time about the dirt, the bugs, the humidity, the sun being too bright, the clouds being too dark, the trees being too tree-like. I asked her about that last one one time and she just waved her hand and was like, "They are too swishy."

I mean, you can't argue with swishy trees.

Katie puts the car in reverse and Eliza suddenly freaks out. "Wait!" she yells. "I forgot my Bible!"

"Too bad. I said five minutes."

And I told you. If Eliza isn't careful, it might end up on her gravestone too.

"Come on, Katie! We are always like ten minutes early! Can't you wait like thirty seconds?"

Katie growls at the clock but pushes on the brake. "You have thirty seconds."

"Thank you!" Eliza is already out the door and running across the street.

Katie grumbles under her breath the entire time Eliza is gone and I hide a smile as I look out the window.

Eliza hops back in the car a minute later, heaving, and Katie points to the clock. "That was way more than thirty seconds."

"It was a minute! Maybe!"

We get to church a few minutes later. Katie dutifully puts her Bible on the aisle seat of the row we pick because Luke will waltz in here halfway through the third song and this is the only way he'll get a seat anywhere close to us.

What is she going to do when she's riding with him?

Actually, it wouldn't shock me if they ended up taking two cars to church.

Eliza is next to Katie, I sit down next to Eliza and the worship band is taking their spots on the stage when Mike steps into the other end of our aisle, next to me.

I scoot down one so that he can go around me and sit next to his sister, but rather than be a normal person and notice this, he sets his stuff down on the other side of me and now it looks like I've purposefully coupled us off away from Katie and Eliza, because there's now an empty seat between me and Mike and Eliza.

I swear, the man is the worst.

"There's a seat for you right here," I hiss to him as the band starts to play.

"I'm fine, thanks," he whispers back.

Now I don't even know what to do. If I scoot back over next to Eliza, it's going to look awfully ridiculous to the people behind us, but if I stay where I am, everyone is going to think Mike and I are an item.

And we definitely are not.

One hundred percent, we are *not*.

"Let's all stand and sing," Kevin, the worship pastor, says into the microphone and the congregation obeys. I stand up and I try to ever so slightly, tiptoe my way back over toward Eliza while we're standing and it's not as obvious.

This is so awkward. And I don't even know why I'm not hopping right back over toward her, other than trying to not appear too mean to the people behind me.

I have got to figure out how to be more confident. I need lessons from Grandma Minnie or something.

Mike is oblivious. He's singing the song quietly and not paying attention to me at all.

Perfect.

Luke, true to form, ambles in right when we are starting up the third song. He gives Katie a kiss on the cheek and then leans over to wave at the rest of us on the aisle. "Good morning!" he whispers.

I smile and wave. Luke might make me crazy with his cardigans and laid-back-ness, but he is really nice. There isn't a mean or selfish bone in his whole body.

By the time the sermon starts, I have half-inched my way back over to the seat next to Eliza and I sit down, breathing a sigh of relief.

There is now no space between me and my friend.

There is also no space between me and Mike, because he sits down in the chair right next to me again.

It's like I'm the middle to a Wakeman sibling sandwich. Like a Wakeman Oreo, only it's the ones they released for awhile where one side was the delicious normal chocolate cookie and the other was that nasty vanilla, flavorless one.

124

I close my eyes and take a deep breath as our pastor comes up on the stage, carrying his well-worn Bible.

"Friends, today is a good day," he says. He says this almost every week and it's always a good reminder for me.

Especially today.

Today is a good day. Today is a good day. Today is a good day.

Maybe if I repeat it enough in my head, it will become true, all Dorothy clicking her heels to go home style.

"Let's start by reading, shall we? Would you open your Bibles with me to Galatians 6?"

It figures.

"'Bear one another's burdens, and thereby fulfill the law of Christ,'" he starts. "And let's skip down a few lines, picking up in verse seven. 'Do not be deceived, God is not mocked; for whatever a man sows, this he will also reap. For the one who sows to his own flesh will from the flesh reap corruption, but the one who sows to the Spirit will from the Spirit reap eternal life. Let us not lose heart in doing good, for in due time we will reap if we do not grow weary. So then, while we have opportunity, let us do good to all people, and especially to those who are of the household of the faith.'"

I think God might be trying to tell me something.

Pastor Mark looks up from his Bible and smiles at all of us. "Have you ever met someone who irritates you?"

It's all I can do to not elbow Mike and gesture all exaggerated like the Beast in *Beauty and the Beast* to Pastor Mark.

"I think we all have that person who immediately comes to our mind. You know the one who makes that spot in the middle of your back ache like when someone is rubbing two pieces of Styrofoam together."

The rest of the congregation, including Mike, is chuckling.

I can't even smile because seriously? This is the sermon? Today of all days when I'm so annoyed by this person and not only is he here but he's sitting right next to me?

This is not funny, Lord.

CHAPTER *Eight*

"Yeah, I'll have the breakfast sandwich combo on a croissant, no mayo, no avocado, no cheese and can I get the bacon on the side? And I want the house barbecue chips with it."

I have been on my feet since five this morning and I've been writing down orders for almost three hours now. I look at my notes and then at the twenty-ish girl at the table in front of me.

"How about I order you eggs and bacon and a croissant on the side?" I offer. "It would save you about four dollars."

She grins at me. "Well, I really am ordering the sandwich combo for the chips."

I can understand this. I would do the same thing. Grandma Minnie's chips are to die for.

Considering the amount of oil and potatoes we go through, many people probably have died for them.

Heart disease and all that. I saw this whole study on how canola oil was basically rancid and Grandma just rolled her eyes and told me to stop reading things online.

"I have lived a good long life, your grandfather has
lived a good long life, your father has lived a good long life.
And goodness knows, I was giving him those chips as
teethers when he was first born."

Then she'd thrown a handful of potatoes in the oil just
to make her point.

I love my grandma.

She is feisty.

"Order the appetizer of the chips for four dollars
because then, they are bottomless," I tell her.

"How about I let you figure out what my order should
be. I want eggs because I feel like I should be a little bit
healthy, a croissant because they are amazing, I love bacon
and I want as many chips as possible."

I make a note and grin at the girl. "I'll take care of
you."

"I appreciate it."

I turn in the table's order to Will, who is barking out
directions like a drill sergeant in charge of a semi-deaf
army. "I NEED BACON. WHERE IS THE BACON?"

My poor cousins. Maybe this is why Grandma and
Grandpa hire from within the family. No one else would take
this kind of abuse over what is really an entry-level job with
crappy pay.

I go back out to my section, armed with a coffeepot
and I refill everyone's cups and return with the iced tea

pitcher. We're in that weird time between breakfast and lunch when customers are split right down the middle between coffee and tea.

I'm pouring the last refill when I see him.

And I don't know if I even see him as much as I know he's here.

I look up and there he is, sitting alone in the corner booth, he's obviously just been seated. And the way he's looking at me, I know he specifically requested that booth in my section.

He holds up his hand in a weird, no-motion wave and I take a deep breath, gripping the iced tea pitcher with both hands and walk over.

"Hey, Ash."

"Hello, Daniel."

Daniel Myers doesn't look a day older, except for maybe a couple of new creases by his eyes. Apparently, Alaska was good to him.

"You're back," I say, trying to come up with something to say since he doesn't really seem in the mood to do much other than smile at me with this sad sort of smile.

"I'm back."

"I thought you weren't ever coming back." Or at least, this was the line I was given when we talked about our future after he said the word "ALASKA".

"I didn't think I was," Daniel says. "Ash, can we talk? I have missed you so much."

"I'm working right now."

"I figured. That's why I came here."

"So, I can't talk now. Grandma will fire me."

Daniel rolls his eyes because he knows that no one has ever really been fired. We've all been threatened, but I think our punishment might be a swat with the wooden mixing spoon on our tush instead.

"You know you won't get fired."

"Daniel, I have eight tables right now. I can't talk. In fact, I've already talked too long. What can I get you to eat?"

I don't know how to react to him sitting here, in person. I mean, he didn't even call or text or email or send a postcard or anything after he left. And he certainly didn't do any of those things before he came back.

You'd think he could have at least sent one lame text. Just one.

How's it going, Ashten?

I mean, that's what? Four words? He couldn't even write four lousy words but he could show up randomly on a Monday during the brunch rush? Are his thumbs broken or something?

By this point, I'm sweating and it's not even hot in here.

"I'll just have coffee."

"Room for cream?" I ask because I'm going to pretend I don't remember how he takes his coffee.

"Please. Ash…"

"I can't right now, Daniel."

"When do you get off work?"

I don't want to tell him so I pretend like another table is calling me and I leave, heart pounding.

I don't even know what to do. There was a point in my life when I would look at Daniel's handsome face and think I was going to see it above a tux, standing at the end of a long aisle, waiting for me to get there in all my white-dressed glory.

And here we are instead. Me, in an apron, hyperventilating while I barely make getting the iced tea into another customer's glass and Daniel sitting all forlorn, in an old, faded sweatshirt, in a booth by himself.

We are a long way from tuxes and dresses.

I walk into the back and Will is calling up one of my orders.

"What's with you?" he barks at me.

"What?"

"You look all pale. You need to get outside more or something."

"I'll keep that in mind." I sigh and start piling the plates on a tray. "Daniel is here."

I don't even know how he heard me, because I muttered it under my breath.

But he obviously does, because he immediately stops, his back straightens and he looks right past me. "Here?" he says and I am suddenly scared for Daniel's life.

"Will."

"Daniel is *here*?" he asks again.

"Daniel?" Mom materializes next to me. "Daniel like your old boyfriend, Daniel?"

"Daniel is here?" My poor dad has joy in his voice, unlike my brother's rage and my mother's curiosity. He wipes his hands on a towel and I can see the excitement in his eyes. "Ashten! Maybe he has seen the light!"

"Not sure they have too much of that in Alaska, Dad."

"What?"

"Light."

Will is already around the counter and I'm grabbing his arm. "Will. Will. *Will.*"

"Stop saying my name. I'm just going to talk to him."

"No, you're not."

"No, I'm not. You don't break my sister's heart and then think you can waltz back in here and get the best food in Missouri afterward. He can leave. We have the right to refuse service to anyone."

"Will…" Mom has her let's-just-smooth-everything-over voice on.

132

"No, Mom. He needs to know he can't get away with it."

I try my best to talk some sense into him. "He's not getting away with it. And good grief." It's not like Will was ever this protective of me when Daniel and I were dating. It shouldn't be different now.

Plus, I'm the older one. I can handle myself. I have been for years.

Maybe not fantastically well, but that's beside the point.

"Settle down, son. We don't want to scare him away."

I'm pretty certain my dad can already see my future children now that Daniel is sitting in the restaurant.

"Look, let's all settle down, okay?" I can't decide who I'm talking to, me or my family. I take a deep breath and try to exhale all slowly like they do in the yoga videos I do sometimes at home.

Not very often. But sometimes. If Katie is gone and the house is totally to myself and it's too cold to be outside, I can sometimes guilt myself into doing a yoga video.

But Katie is rarely gone and I'm rarely home and I'd much rather just go for a run.

Will looks at me and goes back behind the counter. "I'm moving Elise to your section," he says. "You can switch with her."

I don't even argue because part of me knows it's pointless.

"Okay."

"Now, are you sure that's the right call?" Dad asks. "I mean, he could be trying to make amends, Ashten."

"He can try another time, Dad," I say.

"Or not," Will says. "Men don't pick up and leave without weighing all the consequences of their actions. So if he picked up and left, then he's not a real man."

I'm getting *Pinocchio* flashbacks in my head but I stuff them down.

"Besides. Anyone would be nuts to turn down life with you. As annoying as you are and everything." Will gives me a close-mouthed smile and then turns to start yelling at the poor cooks again.

It's as close to a compliment as I've ever heard from Will. "Thanks." I can't decide if I'm touched or not. On the one hand, I think it was a compliment. On the other, he did call me annoying.

I guess I'll take it.

I switch sections with Elise and she has the far back room of the restaurant where a giant family reunion is taking place and I think she sings the hallelujah chorus as she leaves the room.

"Good luck," she says all gleefully, handing me the family's orders. "They all look the same and half of them got sweet tea and half got unsweet. And I've been asked for extra rolls forty-two times."

I nod. Anything sounds better than being in the same room as Daniel right now.

I finally hang up my apron on my little hook in the back at six o'clock. I'm physically and emotionally exhausted. And my feet are killing me.

Whoever invented these super stylish, non-slip shoes for restaurant workers should have added like four times as much padding into the bottom of them.

Will is standing by the door, blocking a yawn with his elbow. "Ready?" he asks.

Apparently, Will is going to walk me out.

Part of me is really touched he's acting like this because Will never acts like this. And part of me is weirded out, because, like I said, he never acts like this.

I nod. "Let me grab my purse." I find it and dig my keys out. We start the trek across the huge parking lot to the last little section for the employees.

The lot is still pretty full, people are coming and going and I'm actually suddenly very thankful that Will is walking me out.

Not that Daniel is a threatening person at all. But it's weird him showing up randomly.

"What are you doing tonight?" Will asks me.

"I'm going to go home and sit," I tell him.

"You moved after Daniel did, right?"

I nod.

"Good. Keep your doors locked. This is creeping me out. Maybe because I just watched one of those Netflix documentaries on domestic violence, but still. He should have at least called."

"My thought too," I say. "Don't worry. First off, he's harmless. Second, he's never been the best at communication, so I'm sure he didn't even think about calling. And third, you worry too much."

"Better paranoid than dead."

"Will, you really need to stop watching those documentaries."

"They are interesting though," Will says, stopping by my car. "Did you see the one about the haunted house?"

"Will, if it doesn't show up in the comedy section or as a made by BBC thing, I generally don't watch it."

"Your loss."

"Or my gain, depending on how much you value a good night's sleep." I smile at my brother. "Hanging out with Everley tonight?"

"We are picking out my ring."

"Fun times." It still really weirds me out that my baby brother is engaged to be married.

I can't decide if it's because there are zero possibilities out there for me or because there's this big part of me that just isn't ready for the family to change. When he gets married, everything is going to be different. Christmases will never be the same, family dinners will never be the same. We will never be able to go grab dinner or coffee after work without having to check with Everley.

And knowing my future sister in law, I think we can go ahead and say that Will and I will never grab coffee or dinner after work again. She can be a little possessive of my brother and his attention.

I get it, don't get me wrong. I don't think there's anything wrong with it. And honestly, things have already been way different between me and Will since he and Everley started dating.

Will gives me a hug and I climb into my car. I have barely hit the lock button when my cell buzzes with a text.

It's Daniel.

So apparently he can text, he just didn't feel like it this last year.

Sorry to make you really flustered today. I really wanted to see you. Can we get coffee after you are off work? I would really like to catch up and see how you are. It was really good seeing you today.

First of all, I felt like I hid my fluster well, thank you very much. Second, I've never seen the word "really" that many times in one text.

I look up and Will's truck brake lights are flashing at the stop sign as he leaves the parking lot.

He would not be happy with me if I went to meet Daniel.

But, on the other hand, he's my little brother and I don't answer to him. I take a deep breath and punch out a quick text. There's a part of me that wants to go home and shower before I meet Daniel, but I'm not going to.

He wants to meet me after work, he will get the Ashten After Work. I smell like the restaurant kitchen and the chicken tortilla soup that I spilled on my leg earlier and my hair is falling out of the bun I had it in and I'm fairly certain that I don't have any makeup still on.

You can only wear makeup for so long going in and out of a steamy kitchen before it melts off your face and puddles on your apron. I've tried using waterproof mascara and it worked way better, but it severely dried out my lashes.

So, I finally figured out that if I put one coat of regular mascara on and then after it dries, add another coat of waterproof. My lashes are happy because they aren't all dried out and I am happy because it stays on.

Still haven't figured out a solution for waterproof eye shadow yet though.

Half the time, I only wear mascara to the restaurant. I'm never really in the mood to do makeup at forty-thirty in the morning anyway.

I get to Starbucks three minutes later and it's the closest one to my house. I sent Eliza and Katie a text, because I'm now paranoid, thanks to my brother.

Hey guys. Meeting my old boyfriend who is apparently back in town at the Starbucks on Wallace. I'm wearing my restaurant clothes still. Black pants, white button down shirt. Just FYI.

As soon as I set my phone down, there's a reply from Eliza.

WHAT THE HECK ARE YOU GIVING US YOUR CLOTHING DESCRIPTION FOR, IS THIS GUY A MURDERER OR SOMETHING?

I mean, we dated for like six months without any sort of incident. I don't know why I'm all freaked out now.

This is all Will's fault.

No, he's fine. He's totally harmless. Will has me all freaked out. Just ignore previous text.

I step out of my car and put my phone in my bag, mostly because I know that Eliza is going to continue to text me. She's apparently off today.

I know Eliza works hard and nursing isn't an easy job, but good grief. I feel like she is always off. And maybe it's because she works a lot of nights, so it seems like she's off a

139

lot, but coming from someone who works twelve hour days a lot of the time, her job seems amazing.

I should have gone into nursing.

It can't be that bad.

And surely there are some nurses who never see blood or vomit or anything coming out the back end of people, because I definitely could not handle any of that.

But I mean, maybe there's like a nurse who primarily works behind a desk, calls other people to come do stuff in an emergency and still does the whole three days on, four days off thing.

I open the door and look around and Daniel isn't here yet. So I order myself a macchiato so there isn't the whole "who pays for this because is it a date or not" awkwardness, take my drink and go sit in one of the big cushy chairs in the corner. There are two of them and it's going to work nicely because then we both have lots of space surrounding us so he hopefully won't be overpowered by the scent of chicken tortilla soup and we aren't having to sit all intimately at a tiny little table, trying not to bump knees the whole time.

"Hey."

I look up and blink for a minute.

"Hi, uh, Mike."

Mike is standing there, holding a cup and sipping it, a slight frown on his face.

140

But, he is often frowning when he's looking at me, so this is nothing new.

"You look tired," he says.

"I am tired."

He sniffs. "Something smells good. Smells like soup. Did Starbucks start selling soup? Every time I come in, the menu is different. Did you know they are selling sub sandwiches now?"

Yes. For like eight dollars a piece.

No, thanks.

Plus, I don't think they are technically sub sandwiches.

"What are you doing?" I ask.

He shrugs. "I come by here pretty often after work. Helps me unwind."

For the life of me, I have no idea what Mike does.

So I decide to ask. Even though, really, I don't care and I should probably be wrapping this up so Daniel doesn't come in while I'm talking with Mike.

"What exactly do you do?"

"I'm in systems management."

"So...you manage systems?"

"People. That's why I have to unwind."

"You don't like people?"

"I prefer systems. That's why I got into this line of work. Then I got a promotion. And now I only manage people." He sits in the chair that I have reserved for Daniel.

"Um," I start, but Mike is still talking.

"People are unmanageable. Especially now with all these workman's rights and workman's this and workman's that. Back when I first started, it was listen to the boss, do what he said and leave work on time. No one ever argued. No one ever tried to call in sick all the time. No one ever tried to use workman's comp for a snowshoeing injury." He takes a long swig of his coffee.

Apparently, Mike has fairly strong feelings about this. Especially since this is the most I have ever heard him say about anything.

Time to wrap it up.

"Well, it was nice running into you," I say, because that's what you say even if you don't actually mean it.

I'm sure Mike is a nice enough person, but I don't see it. I still don't get how sweet Eliza is his sister.

Maybe she got all the nice genes.

"Lots of morons."

And apparently, we are still discussing the job.

"So, it was good to see you." I try again, trying to discreetly check my phone.

Mike looks at me and frowns. This must be his default mode when he's looking at me. "Meeting someone?"

"Actually, yes."

"Katie? Lyzie?"

"No."

He looks at me for a minute and then nods. "Ah. Got it."

"Great to catch up with you." I have no idea how many different ways I have to say this before he finally leaves.

"Well, be careful out there. There are lots of people waiting to prey on clueless women walking around by themselves. Especially after dark."

It isn't dark yet. And I think he just called me clueless.

"I pay attention," I tell him, trying and likely failing from keeping the annoyance out of my tone.

He does one of those little *heh* laughs. "Right. You three are like the worst people in the world at paying attention. I bet I could sit quietly on your couch and it would take you guys a full hour to even notice me there. Never mind how easy it would be to come up behind you in a parking lot. Half the time, Lyzie is so distracted on her phone, she doesn't even remember where she parked."

Now he sounds creepy.

"I'm sure she's careful." Seriously, Mike is never going to stop talking.

"She isn't, that's the thing. None of you guys are. You have to live in the yellow."

I don't know what this means, but it doesn't sound good. Yellow is not my favorite color.

I know it has this reputation of being a happy color, but I think of that saying about eating yellow snow when I hear the word *yellow*. So yeah.

Not my favorite.

The door opens and Daniel walks in then.

He's still wearing his old faded sweatshirt and I'm noticing that his jeans are in pretty ragged shape as well. He's let his hair grow too and it pokes out the back of a baseball cap he smashed on his head since he showed up at the restaurant.

Apparently, Alaska does not have clothing store or barbers.

"Hey Ash."

Mike looks at Daniel and his lips settle into this straight, firm line and I know he's thinking that I met this guy on a street corner somewhere.

"Daniel, this is Mike," I say, standing up and trying to look capable and like I know how to take care of myself.

"Hey," Daniel says.

Mike kind of grunts, looks at me, shakes his head and walks to a table about six feet away, pulling out a chair and sitting so he has his back to the wall and he can see the whole coffee shop.

Good grief.

144

Mike is still eyeing Daniel and Daniel finally looks away and back to me. "Friend of yours?" he asks.

"Eh. Acquaintance."

"Sure about that? He seems a little…"

"Nuts?"

"Yeah."

"He is."

Daniel smiles and turns his chair so his back is to Mike, but I can still see him. Mike pulls a newspaper over and is apparently going to be staying for awhile, even though I could have sworn he was heading out when I walked in.

I watch him pull his phone out of his pocket, look at the screen for a minute, text someone back and shake his head, looking back over at me and Daniel.

Fabulous.

"So." Daniel has his hands clasped between his knees as he leans toward me. "It's good to see you, Ash."

I don't know why but it sort of rankles my nerves when he calls me "Ash". I feel like when you break up and then drop off the face of the earth for over a year, you lose the privilege of using a shortened version of my name.

I kind of force a smile, one, because I'm not sure it's good to see him yet, so I don't want to return the sentiment. Two, because Mike is across the restaurant and as much as he appears to be into the paper, I really doubt he's actually reading it.

This is the most awkward night of my entire life.

"When did you get back?" I ask Daniel.

He takes a breath. "Um, three days ago. I surprised my mom for her birthday."

"So, are you back for good or back for vacation?"

"Back for good."

"Alaska didn't measure up?"

Daniel looks at me. "I really missed everyone here. Especially you."

Mm-hmm. I could tell. All those emails and letters and texts made your point.

"I'm really sorry for the way things were left," Daniel says, rubbing the back of his neck where his hair is curling. "I shouldn't have taken off like that. I don't even have a good excuse."

I shrug, even though it took me a really long time to get over him.

"So, how have you been? Still working at Minnie's in the summer, I see."

I nod. "I'm pretty much the same. I started going to a new church though."

"Oh really?"

I nod again. "And I moved."

"You moved?"

146

"Into a house with a friend."

"Wow."

"Yep."

I look at Daniel and I wait for the hurt and sadness and feelings to come back, but honestly, I don't have them anymore.

I'm a different person than I was a year ago.

And I honestly think Katie and Eliza have a ton to do with that.

Suddenly, I just want to be home, in my sweatpants, hanging out with my best friends.

The conversation lags and it feels awkward. Daniel keeps rubbing the back of his neck, like he feels totally out of place, or maybe it's his hair bugging him.

I have never seen him with such long hair.

His mother probably died when she saw him.

But, he could also be feeling weird because Mike is still here.

Seriously, I don't even know what to do with Mike.

"Well," I say, because we have apparently run out of things to say.

"Yeah, I'm going to get a coffee. Do you need anything else? I bet they have those chocolate scones you always liked."

I don't remember ever ordering a chocolate scone from Starbucks on a date with him, though I do like them. "No, I'm good."

Looks like I'm not leaving anytime soon.

Mike looks over at me while Daniel steps into the line to order and shakes his head all slowly before going back to pretending to read the paper.

This night is the worst.

CHAPTER *Nine*

"Okay, first of all, you may never, *never* text me like that ever again!" Eliza is livid and she's pacing up and down in front of Katie's fireplace, hands on her hips, eyebrows furrowed.

"I said I was sorry," I say, leaning back against the couch. "I don't know what else you want me to say."

"I mean, I was like, she's going a on a date with a murderer! I immediately saw them interviewing me as part of the documentary about you and your poor, unfortunate life and terrible ending. And you know what? I cried. *Cried* as I thought about what they would ask me and what I would have to say and where we would probably find your body. You may not ever do that to me again!"

Needless to say, Eliza isn't really one for exaggeration.

Katie comes in holding a steaming cup of coffee and settles on the couch next to me, tucking her legs up underneath her. "We were worried," she says, all soothingly, likely to try and settle Eliza down. "We care about you a lot."

"I mean, praise God Mike was there," Eliza says.

I look at her. "How did you know that?" I was not about to mention Mike to her or Katie.

The less they hear his name from me, the better as far as future matchmaking attempts go.

"I texted him right away because I knew he was going to be out and he told me he had run into you and he would stay in the Starbucks and make sure everything was okay."

So it's Eliza's fault that Mike never left.

As soon as I stood up to go, Mike closed his newspaper and walked outside right behind us and then I saw him kind of standing by his car, playing with his keys until I had driven out of the parking lot and Daniel had gone out the opposite way.

"Daniel is not a threat," I say. "He's a nice guy. And he's a Christian."

"So, what's with the outfit text?"

"I don't know," I rub my face in my hands and groan. "He showed up all unannounced at the restaurant today and it really threw me off for a little bit and then I mentioned it to Will, who got all freaked out because he's Will and then I don't know. I thought I'd cover the bases. So, I'm sorry, I'll never text you again."

Eliza crosses her arms over her chest and looks at me. "Good."

"Okay."

"All right," Katie says, nodding. "Now, on to more pressing matters, what are we having for dinner?"

"Soup sounds good," I say.

"It is a hundred and twelve degrees with ninety-nine percent humidity outside," Eliza says, rolling her eyes. "No thank you."

"What sounds good to you?" I ask her.

"Ice cream."

Katie is immediately shaking her head. "No, no," she says. "Nope. We are not doing that again. My stomach hurt for two days after we did that."

"It's just frozen milk."

"Well, I need something other than only sugar and dairy in my system." Katie shakes her head. "I'm getting to old. I'm starting to sound like my Gram."

I smile. "I'll have some protein with you."

"Thanks."

Eliza is already looking in the fridge. "You have some chicken breasts in here," she calls.

"Eh. I don't feel like cooking those tonight."

"Eggs?"

"Makes the house smell."

"Peanut butter?"

"Not super filling and I'm really hungry."

Eliza comes back into the living room. "And the ice cream was a bad idea, why?"

I grin. "I'll cook something. I'm sure it's my turn anyway."

"Ash, you've been on your feet since five this morning. I have no excuse. I've been sitting on my tush the whole day."

I have no doubt of this, mostly because since Katie works from home in her sweatpants, she truly does sit on her tush most of the day.

"Speaking of which, I have to go to New York tomorrow late morning for one night," she says, following me into the kitchen.

"That's lame," Eliza says.

"It's going to be so short. I can't believe they still pay these last minute flights for me."

I pull out the chicken and get a skillet going on the stove.

Katie hates raw chicken. Like with all her heart. She can barely look at it.

I think I've been handling raw chicken since I was about four years old. It's a rite of passage in the Wadeley house.

I get out a cutting board, slice the chicken into small strips and start some coconut oil melting in the skillet.

"What are you making?" Eliza asks, plopping onto one of the barstools.

"Chicken."

152

She rolls her eyes. "No, you have to be kidding."

I grin.

I start the chicken cooking in the skillet, wash the cutting board and knife and countertop and then start dicing up tomatoes, shredding lettuce and slicing avocados on another cutting board. I never remember to get the rice started before I start making something like this, so awhile ago, Grandma Minnie taught me this trick about precooking the rice in a pressure cooker in giant batches when you first buy it and then freezing it in quart size freezer bags, so it's always ready to go. I start the rice defrosting, flip the chicken and season it with salt, pepper, a little bit of garlic powder and onion powder. When the chicken is done, I pull it out, add more oil to the hot pan and then sauté some frozen stir fry vegetables really quick.

The rice is done, the chicken is done, the veggies take no time at all and we are sitting down with bowls of goodness a few minutes later. Grandma Minnie started bottling and selling her legendary chicken sauce years ago, so I pull that out of the fridge and warm some up to serve at the table on top of our bowls. It's basically a blend of soy sauce, tiny bit of garlic, raspberry preserves and a lot of sugar, but it's amazing.

"I even feel healthy now," Eliza says, crunching a bit of lettuce, veggies and chicken.

"That's because it is pretty healthy. I mean, basically everything is except the sauce."

Eliza douses more on her chicken. "Yeah, but the sauce is amazing."

"It really amazing. What is in this?"

"Can't tell. It's a family secret. But if you're allergic to raspberries, it might be a long night."

The girls grin.

Katie shakes her head. "I don't even know how you manage to keep secrets with how big your family is. What do you do? Swear them to secrecy at birth?"

"Eh, it's like a rite of passage if you want to start working at the restaurant. Which most of us either do or have done at some point in our lives. So, at some point, yes, most of us are sworn to secrecy."

I think there have maybe been three of my cousins who haven't worked there, so I guess they can reveal any secrets they want to. But if you don't work at the restaurant, you usually don't know the secrets anyway.

Although, most of my family uses Grandma Minnie's recipes for normal life cooking.

Like me just now. Grandma serves this on a plate and usually piles steaming, grilled chicken tenders on a plate, douses them in the special sauce and serves it with rice, grilled corn on the cob and buttered broccoli.

It's one of our most popular dishes right after Christmas for the healthy-food-like quality.

Though, I don't know that I would actually consider buttered broccoli healthy.

One year, Will tried to talk us into serving "earth bowls" in the diner in January and after campaigning hard for over six months, he finally got the green light for one month of a trial. He had to document the cost per bowl to make, the amount of bowls consumed and the ingredients that went to waste.

I'd never even heard of earth bowls before Will wanted to introduce them, so I went and tried one when I had Martin Luther King Jr. Day off in January.

It was awful. Like seriously, it tasted like nothing. And it totally did not have the Minnie's Diner feel that people are used to getting. Minnie's isn't known for their flair, but they are known for the comfort food.

Earth bowls are not comfort food. It was basically a big pile of lettuce, barely blanched broccoli, tomatoes, corn and I think walnuts. There was some sort of homemade vinaigrette on the top and it was super runny and gross.

Needless to say, those were not back by popular demand the next year. I think we lost money on all the ingredients spoiling.

If anything, I half expected to see picketers in front of the diner when I went back the next weekend.

Eliza and Katie are inhaling their bowls and Eliza disappears while Katie is doing the dishes and comes back carrying a half-gallon of ice cream, a jug of Hershey's syrup and a Tupperware container filled with fresh, mixed fruits.

"This is the best part of the summer," she declares.

"Ice cream?" I grin.

"And fresh berries."

She pulls out three bowls and starts making some amazing looking sundaes while Katie and I finish cleaning the kitchen. True to form, the girls both brew themselves a cup of coffee and then take their ice cream into the family room and sit on the couches. I find a peach Snapple in the back of the fridge and sit down next to Eliza.

"Sorry for yelling at you today," she says, elbowing me. "I just love you a lot."

"I love you a lot too. Try not to worry about me. I can take care of myself."

"Yeah, but you shouldn't have to all the time."

"I don't all the time. Grandma Minnie feeds me a lot too. It's why I have hips."

Katie rolls her eyes and then licks her spoon. "So, tell me about Daniel. Is he cute?"

I think about Daniel and then about Luke and Cooper. I know their types and so no, they would not think that Daniel was very cute.

He's a little too rough for them, I think. Luke is almost verging on hipster-like. He often wears plastic-framed glasses and his jeans are definitely in the realm of skinny. Cooper isn't quite like that, but he's very polished and stylish and clean-cut.

Daniel is not any of those things. Especially now with his hair longer. He looks like he walked out of a cabin in the middle of a mountain range. He's always had a beard as long as I've known him. And I've rarely, if ever, seen him out of his hiking boots.

He was born to live in Alaska. Or Colorado or somewhere like that.

So it's weird to me that he's back.

"He's...I don't know."

"Why did you guys break up?" Eliza asks, eating a spoonful of ice cream and berries. "And how long did you date?"

"Around six months and he moved to Alaska."

Katie nods. "Yeah, I could see how that would put a little bit of a damper on things."

"Did you see it going somewhere?" Eliza asks.

I feel like I'm at an age where I'm not going to date someone for the sake of dating someone. Though, honestly, I was never really in that camp in the first place. If I don't like you enough to potentially marry you, I'm not going to be dating you.

"I mean, yes," I say, shrugging. "I wouldn't have been dating him if I hadn't."

"Did you know he was considering moving to Alaska?"

I shake my head. "No. He'd told me a couple of times how he thought it was the most beautiful state and he'd love to go there, but I always thought he meant like on a cruise or something."

Thinking about Daniel and who he is, though, I should have known he's not the cruise type. He's totally the type to find some abandoned cabin in the woods and live there, sleeping with a shotgun in case a bear breaks in.

I guess I should have seen it coming.

"So, was there any chemistry or anything today?" Eliza asks.

Eliza is funny. Before Katie started dating Luke, there were a few other guys on the horizon and Eliza was so worried that Katie was going to settle for someone she didn't have any chemistry with. "Spark is important," she was constantly saying.

But then, when all of us could see the giant, glowing ember of a spark between her and Cooper, she totally denied it. I mean, complete strangers were basically complimenting their chemistry and she still didn't get it.

I guess she eventually came around.

Apparently, she is putting herself on Spark Patrol for me too.

Well, she has her work cut out for her.

To my knowledge, I've never had that *feeling* with anyone. Ever. Not Daniel now, not Daniel then. And really, Daniel's the first guy I've ever seriously dated. I went on a few sporadic dates here and there in college but nothing that was worth writing home about.

Not that I really have to write home, since I live here, but you get what I mean. And not that I would write home ever because my poor Dad couldn't take that kind of letter over and over again. I fully plan on telling Dad when it's serious enough for us to be doing ring shopping. And hopefully not before.

All that to say, I think there's probably some people who think spark is extra important, but I am not one of those people. Sure, I think you should be attracted to the person. But basing everything on this indefinable quality that most people can't even really describe doesn't make sense. I guarantee that most couples don't feel a lot of spark when they are up with the stomach flu together or dealing with a sick kid in the middle of the night.

I shrug at Eliza. "I don't think so."

"Eh, I say to end it now," she says, scraping her bowl. "Send him packing back up to Alaska. Maybe he can find a good snow dog team if he's that lonely."

Katie perks up. "That was a great movie."

"Only because Paul Walker was adorable," Eliza says to her. She looks at me. "He's not Paul Walker adorable, is he? Because I'm pretty sure that every woman on the planet had some sort of spark with him in that movie."

"Definitely not."

"Eh," she says again. "Toss him back."

"He's not a fish, Eliza," Katie says, rolling her eyes.

"Isn't that the saying, though? 'There's more fish in the sea'? There are so many fish in the sea. You never have to keep one that is all creepy like those deep sea fish. Be like me. I avoided those guys and went straight for Flipper."

I snort. Katie loses it.

Eliza grins. "I'm just saying."

CHAPTER *Ten*

The week goes by in a blur of my alarm going off at four in the morning, taking orders and refilling coffees.

I make enough money teaching that I don't need to do this to myself. So why do I do it to myself?

"Ash, you are a life saver," Grandma Minnie said to me as I left last night. "I don't know how we manage during the school year without you. You have no idea how much I appreciate you giving up your summers for us."

I mean, the appreciation was sweet. And I know Grandma Minnie and Grandpa John have this huge heart for us, their grandkids, and the legacy they are leaving behind. Grandpa is forever coming into the kitchen and looking at all of his grandkids working and getting this huge, proud smile on his face.

So there's that.

I guess I'll keep going back.

Today is my day off, but my eyes still pop open at four in the morning, even though I definitely turned off every alarm possible before I fell into bed last night.

It's Friday and I'm going to sleep in.

I roll over, pull the covers up to my chin and close my eyes tight.

Go to sleep. Go to sleep. Go to sleep.

Nothing.

Maybe I should take a line from one of my favorite all time Christmas movies and "count my blessings instead of sheep".

I think it might work better if Bing and Rosemary came and sang to me, instead.

I finally give up on going back to sleep at 4:45 in the morning and just get up, pulling my robe on and going across the hall to brush my teeth.

I look at the Keurig when I get to the kitchen and almost make myself a cup of coffee. If I were to ever drink the stuff, it would be now, first thing in the morning before my brain is really remembering how much I don't like it.

But I don't. I pour myself a bowl of cereal and a small glass of cranberry apple juice and sit down at the table.

I look at my bran cereal and my juice and the time.

I am like eighty years old.

"Ash?" Katie stumbles in, eyes closed against the kitchen light.

"Go back to bed," I say, half because she obviously needs to and half because I don't want her to come to the same realization and worry she's living with some form of Benjamin Button or that girl that Blake Lively played in whatever movie that was about the lady who stopped aging when she was twenty-something but was like a hundred years old really.

Katie squints at me, shadowing her face with her hands. "I thought you were off today?"

"I am. I couldn't sleep."

"Me neither."

"You look like you were asleep."

"Well, I mean, I was, but then I saw the light from under my door and was worried you were on your way to work when you weren't supposed to go."

I smile. Katie is such a good roommate.

"I'm good. I'm hungry so I decided to get breakfast. You should go to bed though."

Unlike me, who goes to bed usually by ten, especially on the night I've worked, Katie is never in bed before midnight. Ever.

She's one of those people who gets this huge second wind right when I am passing out on the couch. I think I was in bed by eight-thirty last night.

Which might also be why I can't go back to sleep. Maybe the issue isn't that Bing and Rosemary aren't here.

"You should try watching the Barefoot Contessa," Katie says to me.

"Why? So I can be sad about my cereal?"

"No, her voice is very soothing. She always puts me to sleep."

I grin. "I was wishing for Bing Crosby and Rosemary Clooney to come sing to me."

"Oh, that's a great movie." Katie immediately livens up. "Let's watch that!"

I look at her, crunching my cereal. "Right now?"

"Why not?"

"Because it's not even five in the morning," I say. "And that's a Christmas movie."

She shrugs. "It always feels more like winter before the sun comes up anyway." She walks over, flips the switch for the gas fireplace and the flickering glow fills the living room with it's happy dance. She nods to the couch and throws one of her thick, fuzzy blankets to the other side of it. "I'll even let you have the side with the end table," she grins.

I carry my cereal and juice over to the couch and she gets the movie queued up on Netflix.

It starts with the war scene and Bing singing the title song, "White Christmas". It's a little weird to be sitting here in front of a fire watching a Christmas movie in the middle of the summer.

But, Katie is right. The darkness helps a little. Maybe because the air conditioner ran all night so it is actually a tiny bit chilly in our house.

I look over during the classic "Snow" song and Katie is dead asleep on the couch, all curled up in a little ball under the blanket. I smile.

When the movie ends, I tiptoe over and lightly pat her shoulder until her eyelashes start fluttering and she lifts her head all confused. "Go back to bed, friend," I say, because it's only around 6:30.

"What time is it?"

"Not even seven."

"Oh good." She sits up straight and rubs her eyes. "Gosh, I love that movie."

I grin. "How much did you actually see?"

"I think I saw them become Wallace and Davis."

"Mm-hmm. You should go back to bed."

She shakes her head. "I can't. I have a seven o'clock meeting in New York."

"You were just there." She got back after midnight on Wednesday. Thankfully, Eliza offered to pick her up at the airport. I had to leave the house by four-thirty yesterday morning so there was no way I could have picked her up and then worked a full day. Katie was planning on driving herself until Eliza talked her into being picked up.

"I don't like you on the roads that late after you've been traveling all day," she'd said to Katie.

"Aren't you going to be on the roads after working all day? I think the vast majority of people would agree that it's way harder to work as a nurse for twelve hours than to sit in a taxi and an airplane."

"After working."

"Sorry. Sit in a conference room, then in a taxi, then in an airplane."

Somehow, Eliza had still won the argument.

It's not shocking. Eliza often wins arguments. It's because volume usually trumps logic.

Something my Grandma Minnie has perfected over the years.

Sometimes I think it would be really entertaining to watch Eliza and Grandma Minnie in the same room together. I need to bring my friends to family dinner sometime.

"I know, but one of the people I needed to meet with wasn't around, so we are doing a video conference. So I'm glad I got up. Thanks for waking me up. I doubt I could hear my alarm out here."

"Don't doubt too much." I've heard Katie's alarm through her closed door, the hallway, my closed door and over the air purifier I keep by my bed purely for the white noise.

The girl has to be hard of hearing after having that blare in her ear every morning.

She leaves to go make herself presentable and get a cup of coffee before her meeting. Katie often works on the couch, but when I'm around or when she has a video conference, she uses the office.

She comes back out a few minutes later and she's got her hair done, her makeup on and she's wearing a pretty navy blue top and pajama pants.

"Nothing like only having to get half dressed," I grin at her.

"You're just jealous you don't get to dress like this for your work," Katie says.

"Honestly, it would probably be easier with the third graders," I say.

She grins, pops a cup under the Keurig, adds her sugar and cream and then waves as she goes into the office. "See you in a few hours, friend."

The office door clicks behind her and I look at the clock. Almost seven.

So sad that I've already been up for two hours.

I go take a long, hot shower and by the time I'm done with the whole applying leave-in conditioner, slowly combing out my hair and drying with the diffuser routine, it's almost eight o'clock.

Especially in the summer, I can get really lazy about my hair. Mostly because I spent an hour getting it and my makeup to look as perfect as it can get, but I know the moment I open my door and the humidity touches my hair, it's going to spring up like I've touched an electrical outlet. Sometimes, I can almost hear the "boing!"

I'd estimate that a good ninety-five percent of the summer is spent with my hair up in a high, curly bun.

I can hear Katie on her conference call and so I get dressed and go out to my car. It's a beautiful summer day and I'm about to become the lamest person on the planet and go back to my workplace on my day off.

But Grandma Minnie always served peach pancakes on Friday mornings and that sounds amazing right now. My breakfast cereal isn't filling me up very long, which is in direct contrast to what the box said about it.

Plus, after watching *White Christmas*, I want Grandma's spiced tea and since it's summer, I don't have any in the pantry.

But Minnie's Diner always serves it year round. Just like hot chocolate. Which I would drink if I liked any other hot drinks than Grandma's spiced tea.

"Aren't you off?" My cousin, Ellen, is hostessing today and she looks down behind her little station, probably checking the staff list for the day.

"I'm off. Just wanted some pancakes. And yes, I know."

"Lame," Ellen sing-songs, grinning at me.

"I know, I know."

"Go ahead and seat yourself. Unless you're going to sit in the back."

168

I look over her shoulder at the seating chart. A two top table is available in Meg's section, so I mark myself down with the dry erase marker and head that way. It's only a little after eight, but the restaurant is already pretty packed.

But I guess it's Friday and Fridays are usually more full.

"Hey," Meg appears in front of me. "How's it going, Ash?"

"Good."

"Are you going to family dinner this week?"

"Was planning on it."

"Okay good." She grins at me. "I'm bringing Mark."

"Mark the new guy Mark?"

"Right. He's so sweet. You will love him." Meg is sighing and dreamy-eyed and I kind of want to shake my head, but I don't and I instead muster up whatever happiness I can from the depth of my soul and actually try to appear glad for her.

"Oh good!" I say and there enough cheese in my voice that Grandma Minnie won't have to send out for any to use in the omelets today.

I love Meg, but the girl has fallen in love what...like thirty-two times in the last three years? I've met more guys than I can count.

I think this might be Mark 2 or Mark 3.

Either way, he's not the first Mark I've ever met with her at Family Dinner.

"So, what are you wanting? Super lame that you're here on your day off, by the way."

"Yeah, thanks. Peach pancakes, please. And hot spiced tea."

"Regular, chai or peppermint?"

"Do we do peppermint spiced tea not around Christmas?" I ask, frowning.

"Probably not but I'm sure I can find peppermint somewhere if you're really set on it."

"Mm. Just regular." I'm not big on all the additional flavors Grandma has come up with over the years. Plain and simple.

I guess that's me.

"Whipped cream on the pancakes?"

I sigh. I'm sitting here alone at my work on my one day off.

"Why not," I say.

"Goodness knows you need to continue to live for something," Meg says, writing it down on her pad. "Might as well be whipped cream."

"You are extra encouraging."

"No worries. See you in a few."

I brought a new novel I've been wanting to read with me, so I open it and read through the dedication. Most people I know skip those pages entirely, but I really love seeing what the authors have to say about their books.

To Dee. May you find your way like Piper.

Well. That was good and cryptic. Who is Dee? Why is she lost? And I'm assuming I'll find out about Piper in the story, but still. Weird way to start.

I really hope this isn't one of those Appalachian Trail books or something like that where the lady gets lost in the wilderness and has to find herself. Literally and figuratively.

"Hey! Ashten!"

I look up and Eliza is waving at me from across the room. She's holding a cup of coffee with her other hand and Mike is at the table with her, sipping his and nodding to me.

Well, now I have to go say hi.

So much for finding out about Piper and why she's lost and how Dee is similar to her.

"Hey, guys," I say, walking over.

Eliza immediately pulls out one of the empty chairs at their table. "Hi! Sit! How are you?"

She is basically bouncing and I think Tigger might need to lay off the caffeine. Based on the way that Mike is looking at her, I think he agrees with me.

"Good. Tired. And here on my one day off," I say, because it's better if you announce your lameness instead of waiting for people to put two and two together. Especially if one of those people is pretty judgy and one of them is extra loud.

"Psh," Eliza waves a hand. "This place is the best! I'd come here every day whether I worked here or not, too! What did you get to eat?"

"Pancakes. And spiced tea."

"Wait, you got a hot drink?" Eliza is aghast.

"It's the only one I like."

"Not a coffee drinker?" Mike asks me.

I shake my head and he nods, raising his eyebrows, sipping his coffee.

"Glad there's at least one of you who abstains. Eliza drinks enough for the rest of us."

Eliza rolls her eyes. "And I'll thank you to never use that sentence out of context."

Mike smiles over his coffee cup.

Meg is back with my spiced tea and she looks around before spotting my wave. "Found some friends?" she asks and I cringe at how lame I sound.

I guess in Meg's eyes though, I probably am pretty lame. I'm in my thirties now, I'm still not married, I still don't have kids and I still work at this restaurant.

Meg is twenty-two, has been through who knows how many boyfriends, will probably get married in the next couple of years and wants to move as far away from Carrington Springs as she possibly can.

172

"Thanks," I say when she sets the cup in front of me.

"Sure. Your breakfasts will be out shortly." She flashes a toothily grin at Mike and twirls to leave.

And maybe things aren't super serious with Mark 3. Personally, I wouldn't bring anyone to Family Dinner unless there was already a ring on my finger. Too much chance that things could go south and quickly. There are usually no less than sixty-five people there and often more. And everyone is loud and overwhelming and opinionated.

Best to save that part of my life for later.

Eliza watches her go and slightly shakes her head. Mike seems completely oblivious to the flirtation.

"How old is she?" Eliza asks me in a low voice.

"Twenty-two, I think."

Eliza rolls her eyes. "She's just a baby. She needs to find herself someone other than Grandpa here."

Mike frowns at her. "I can hear, you know. Passed it with flying colors at my last checkup."

"*And* you just made my case," Eliza says, slapping the table. "No one in their twenties talks about 'their last checkup'."

"I'm not in my twenties."

"You can say that again."

"You act like thirty-two is so much younger than thirty-six, but it's really not."

Eliza waves a hand. "I am in my *young* thirties. You, my friend, are on the downhill slope to forty. Skiing down, the wind whizzing through your ever-thinning hair." She pretends to hold ski poles and makes a little *schoop schoop* sound as she leans right and left.

I laugh.

Mike sips his coffee and shakes his head, but I can tell he's trying to hide a smile. There's a very sweet, gentle expression that comes into his eyes when he's looking at his sister. "My hair is fine, thank you," he says. "I think I'm going to be gray before I'm bald."

"Well, praise God for that. The Wakemans have weird shaped heads."

"We do not."

"Dude. Have you seen our baby pictures?" Eliza sighs and looks at me. "I seriously look like E.T."

I smirk.

"You did not," Mike says. "I mean, don't get me wrong, you were pretty discolored and wrinkly, but I think we can blame jaundice and being born four weeks early for that. As soon as you started gaining weight, you looked fine."

"Speaking as a nurse, we have abnormal cranial circumferences."

He rolls his eyes. "Good try."

She grins.

I quietly sip my tea and watch the two bicker. It's kind of fun to observe them. Will and I never had this kind of relationship. A little bit maybe in high school, but then he started dating and getting serious about the restaurant business and there wasn't time to hang out anymore.

Plus, I know Mike and Eliza have a completely different relationship since it has been just the two of them for so long.

Mike is completely different around Eliza. I don't know what it is. Maybe it's that he doesn't have the semi-permanent wrinkle between his eyes that makes him constantly look fed up with you and life in general.

Meg is back with our breakfasts. Eliza's French toast is covered in a layer of blueberry sauce and then a powdered sugar snowfall. My pancakes have basically eaten the plate and the mountain of whipped cream on top is tall enough for a good sized rat to sled down.

Eliza and I both look at the plate Meg sets in front of Mike and it's really bare. Two eggs, sunny side up. Two slices of turkey bacon. And a cup of our seasonal fruit, which right now, is basically everything. Honeydew, watermelon, strawberries, blueberries and raspberries.

Meg leaves with a promise to return to check on us, but really, I know that she's not coming back because she's going to assume that I will go get whatever we still need.

"Yours looks sad," Eliza says to Mike.

"Tell me that when I outlive the both of you by twenty years," Mike says. "My BMI is better just looking at my plate."

"Yeah, but mine has antioxidants," Eliza says, poking the blueberry sauce and licking the end of her fork.

"Right. You keep telling yourself that."

"And it goes better with my chocolate macadamia nut coffee." Eliza grins. "But, I guess yours probably goes better with your black-as-your-soul coffee. You should probably pray since we are apparently closer to seeing Jesus than you are."

I grin. Mike shakes his head.

CHAPTER *Eleven*

I follow Eliza back home. Mike headed into his work. I guess he can schedule when he's going to be there or not, because we don't even get back to our house until a little before ten.

Such a weird breakfast. Mike seemed normal. Relaxed. Possibly even funny.

So different than I've ever seen him.

Eliza walks across the street, swinging her keys around her finger when I get out of the car. Katie's car isn't in the garage, so I'm assuming she packed up and went to her other office, the place most people call Panera.

"Don't you ever work anymore?" I ask Eliza.

"Sure! I worked last night."

I will never understand how she can be this functional on no sleep. When I was about seventeen, I talked my parents into keeping this puppy that randomly showed up at our house and the dog never slept. I mean, never slept. It barked and whined and cried the entire night in it's little kennel and I was about to lose it every night, but especially every morning when I would have to get up after getting no sleep and function for the rest of the day at school.

It took me all of about six days before I found a friend at school who wanted a dog and seemed okay with the idea of never sleeping. As far as I know, the dog lived a long, happy life with her.

And I got to sleep.

Eliza is amazing.

"Aren't you tired?"

She shrugs. "I'm used to it. I'll take a nap in a little bit. I'm working again tonight, so I try to simulate a normal schedule as best as I can. I got off at seven, so I'll go to bed in about three hours and try to sleep until about five so I have time to grab a meal before I go back to the hospital. The biggest thing is figuring out what to eat when I wake up from my nap, since it's technically my breakfast but also my dinner and it needs to be filling enough that I can make it for awhile without eating, since I rarely get a long enough break to eat for the first part of my shift."

I do not envy night nurses. Even though I slightly envy the three days on, rest of the week off thing.

Maybe I can work something out like that for teaching. I'll teach Monday through Wednesday and then be off until Monday again.

Though I think three straight twelve hour days of my third graders would be enough to make me never want to have children. There's a reason the school day is only six and a half hours.

Plus my prep and grading time.

Which I prefer to do at home, in my jammies, in front of *Gilmore Girls*.

"So." Eliza smiles at me.

"So?"

"What do you think about Mike?"

"Oh my gosh."

"What?" Eliza protests. "He's cute, he's single...he's very single. He has a good job, he loves Jesus and he's smart. What else do you want?"

I kind of growl out a sigh and walk into the house. Eliza follows me, still talking.

"I want you guys to be happy and I don't see how this isn't perfect. I love you, I love him. Plus," she says, holding her hands up excitedly when the get to the kitchen and I turn to face her, "Plus, if you marry Mike, we will be *sisters*."

Immediately, the song from *White Christmas* starts playing through my head and I don't know why I thought it was such a fun idea to watch that movie this morning.

That song is the worst.

Mostly because it will now be stuck in my head for the next five months. Which gives me, what, a month before it's back in my head thanks to Katie and Eliza watching *White Christmas* on repeat all Christmas season long.

Although, I guess they will both be married by then, so maybe I won't.

Now I'm sad. I shake my head slightly to get back to the conversation.

"Eliza," I start.

"All I want to hear is that you'll think about it."

"I don't have to think about it, I already know."

Eliza gapes. "How could you already know? You barely know the man."

"He's not my type," I tell her.

She shakes her head and starts counting the points off on her fingers. "Smart, good-looking, loves Jesus, has a job..." she shrugs, looking at her hand. "Yeah, just those alone, I guess I can see why he's not your type."

"Eliza."

"No, seriously! How is he not your type? Was the Eskimo your type?"

"What?"

Eliza waves her hand. "David, Darrell, Dawson. Whatever his name was who moved to the Arctic."

"Darrell?" I look at her and slowly shake my head. "*Daniel*."

"Right."

"And it was Alaska."

"That's the one."

I take a deep breath and rub my temples.

Maybe I do need to start drinking coffee. Goodness only knows that I need some sort of caffeine to deal with Eliza and her thought circus.

I have heard from several different people at several different events what an amazing nurse Eliza is. A few people from church have had her when they delivered their babies, a few of her fellow nurses go to a Bible study with us and one of the doctors on her floor goes to our church too. And all of them rave about Eliza and her steel trap mind and her competency and how she's the best nurse to ever live, right behind Florence Nightingale.

I love Eliza with all my heart and I would love to see Work Eliza. Because Home Eliza can talk circles around me.

Supposedly, at work, she actually listens to the patients.

Maybe if I were having a baby, Eliza would pay attention to what I'm saying right now.

"So?" Eliza is waiting for me to talk and I have no idea what she asked me.

"What?"

"What does Damian have going for him?"

I cover my face and yell. "Dear goodness!"

"Sorry!" Eliza is equally as loud. "Derek?"

"Daniel. *Daniel.*"

"Right. That's the one. How is he more your type? Does he have a job that isn't in Antarctica? Does he love

Jesus enough to put his significant other above his own personal feelings about relocation? Does he know the value of a haircut?"

And apparently, Mike told Eliza about Daniel's current hair state, because I don't remember mentioning the long hair to her.

I can't say I'm surprised. Eliza probably demanded a play by play of what Mike saw at Starbucks. She can be very demanding.

Maybe it's a family trait.

I look at her. "Daniel is a nice guy," I say.

"And?"

"And that's it. It's not anything anymore. Just because he's back doesn't mean we are going to start dating again. But really, Eliza, you have got to lay off of me and Mike. It's not going to work. Our personalities would not mesh very well."

"So you don't find him attractive at all?"

I think about Mike and while there have been times where I thought he seemed okay, the times when I've been completely annoyed or offended or fed up with him have far outnumbered the good times. "Sorry."

She looks at me and sighs. "Fine."

"Thank you."

She's quiet for a minute. "So."

"So."

"Want to go with me to look at flowers?"

This is Missouri, so it's greenish, but it's also like an oven outside right now and my hair can't handle anymore humidity than the walk from the car to the air conditioning. Even the walk from the car to the restaurant this morning made me give up and pull it into this ponytail on the top of my head that looks more like a pile of out of control curls than a ponytail.

When I hear the word *ponytail*, I usually picture like Cher from *Clueless* and her straight, blonde, perfect hair.

Unachievable.

At least for me.

I look at Eliza. "Like in a field?"

"Like at a florist? For the wedding?"

"Oh," I draw the word out. "I thought you were taking a nap?"

"Not until later. Want to come with me? There's one in particular I want to check out today. Got really good reviews on Google."

I don't have any other plans other than maybe putting on sweatpants and working on my finances, so I shrug and nod. "Sure." I don't mind shopping, especially when it's not my money we are spending.

I'm so close to having enough for my down payment, it's a little bit scary. So far, it's been this really lofty goal for forever and now that the numbers are starting to show the final stretch, I'm alternating between really excited and really terrified.

It's good Katie is getting married. She still hasn't said anything about me leaving, but I can read the writing on the wall.

Luke lives in the crappiest apartment known to man, according to Katie, so obviously, he's going to move into Katie's adorable, super clean, super cute, basically model-ready home.

Sometimes, I wonder what life is going to look like for the two of them when kids enter the picture. I'm around kids every single work day for nine months of the year and I feel like I can say this with a lot of authority: Kids are gross.

Like legitimately gross.

I have a feeling it might change Katie a little bit.

I grab a water bottle, fill it with water from the fridge and follow Eliza back outside and across the street to her house. She climbs into the driver's seat and I slide in next to her.

"What are your thoughts on tulips?"

"I think they are pretty. They remind me of spring. And they are always really beautiful, rich colors."

Eliza nods to me. "See? Thank you. That's all I was looking for. I asked Cooper the same question and he said, 'I think two lips are better than one.'"

I snort.

184

"Anyway. I'm thinking since it's a November wedding, we should go with kind of fall themed flowers. Katie is getting married right before me, so I really don't want to do a copycat wedding and I know she's going with a lot of whites and creams. She told me her goal is to have an oatmeal colored wedding."

I smile. I can totally see that. Katie's house is oatmeal colored too. Why wouldn't her wedding be those same colors? She loves whites and creams and very light beiges. She's the poster child for the white-washed farmhouse look everywhere on Pinterest right now.

Then there's Eliza who definitely painted her master bedroom a neon-ish teal a few weeks ago.

Somehow, she makes it work. But the differences between the two houses always make me laugh.

I'm curious what I'll do in my own house. I feel like in a lot of ways, I'm like the mid-range of both of my friends. I like the white, but I like splashes of the crazy colors, like the bright, teal throw pillows that Eliza has.

I just don't think I could do the red wall too.

We get to the florist and Eliza walks in, inhaling. "I love the way these places smell. In another life, I would have been a florist."

"Instead you picked a career in what a lot of people consider the worst smelling place on earth. A hospital."

"Eh," Eliza waves my comment off. "Those people never went on a field trip to a sewage plant. My eighth grade teacher was a little bit of a free spirit. Hello!" she says, all friendly and chipper to the employee in a dark green apron who walks out then. "I'm Eliza, this is my friend Ashten and I'm the one who called earlier today about checking out wedding bouquets."

"Oh yes, hello." The lady reminds me of that housekeeper lady on *The Brady Bunch*. "I'm Eleanor. Come right this way." She shows us to a table in the middle of the shop and nods for us to sit down. "What we usually do is have you look through some of our previous work so we can get an idea what you are looking for and then we will design a custom floral package for you."

Eliza is nodding. The lady hands her a three ring binder and she scoots closer to me so I can see the pictures too.

"Oh wow," she says to the first one. It's a huge bouquet, with like a waterfall effect and it drops almost all the way to the floor.

"This is our Grand Cathedral arrangement," Eleanor says.

"It's amazing," Eliza says.

It's a little too much for my taste, but I know my role as bridesmaid, so I smile and nod.

Eliza grins at me. "You hate it."

186

"I did not say that."

"Please. I can read you like a book, Ashten Wadeley. You do not like this." She turns to Eleanor. "It's a little too much for me, but I think it's gorgeous." She turns the page and the next one is very simple. White roses straight cut on the ends and tied together with a ribbon.

"This one is our Simple Elegance look," Eleanor says.

"This is totally—"

"Katie," I say with Eliza and she nods.

"Totally. Like she designed it herself."

"We'll have to send her over here."

Eliza looks up at Eleanor. "My other bridesmaid who is also engaged."

"I see."

We flip through the book and Eliza finds a couple she likes. My favorite was the bouquet that looked like someone pulled over to the side of the road and picked a bunch of wildflowers. Bright, cheerful. It looked exactly like Eliza.

I don't say anything though, because I am not about to sway her.

"So, I have a favorite," Eliza says, when she gets to the end.

"Great! Which one?"

"The wildflower one."

I grin.

Eliza smiles at me. "And you obviously approve."

"I think it's beautiful and it looks just like you," I nod.

"Perfect," Eleanor says.

"So we are getting married November 18th," Eliza says. "I would really love some fall colors in the flowers. Maybe sunflowers? Or like some orange-y stuff?"

Eleanor is nodding and she stands. "Let me pull a few flowers for you and we can go from there."

"Sounds great!"

Eleanor leaves and Eliza looks over at me. "Well, that was nice and easy. If planning a wedding was all like this, I would go into the biz."

I think about Eliza as a wedding planner and get what is probably considered heart palpitations. I don't think that super creative people should work in creative fields. Just like I don't think people who natural slant toward a more leadership role should ever be teachers.

It never ends well for either one and they end up broken-spirited and impoverished on the side of the road.

Or at least sad.

"I think you are probably where you should be," I tell her.

Eliza grins. "You are funny, Ashten Wadeley. And I'm glad you're my friend."

I smile back at her. "Me too." And I am. As crazy as she is, my life would be a lot less colorful without Eliza in it.

Friday night, I'm looking at the Bible on my lap, arms crossed over my chest.

I have a feeling I've been going about this confidence thing all wrong.

Maybe, the confident access has less to do with actual confidence and more to do with *feeling* confident.

Like, the whole fake it until you make it thing. You know? Basically the Christian version of dressing for the job you want.

So, maybe, if I portray myself as this confident woman, I'll stop feeling so awkward.

This could work.

CHAPTER *Twelve*

Saturday morning, I'm back to pouring coffee for approximately seven hundred and twelve people who are all seated in my section at Minnie's Diner.

I might be slightly exaggerating.

But still. There is not an empty chair anywhere, except for the one smashed into the barely big enough space between two tables because it got pulled out of the way for a highchair.

This is insanity.

Grandpa John and Grandma Minnie are going to have to add on to this building.

Again. It would make like the eighth or ninth expansion.

I guess, though, it would be more my parents or Will heading up that project.

I go in the back to get another pitcher and check on my orders and Grandma Minnie is rolling out biscuit dough and flipping them onto the giant cookie sheets like a machine.

The woman is amazing. She's eighty years old.

When I am eighty, I do not want to be making biscuits for a packed restaurant.

"Need any help, Grandma?" I ask her, walking past.

"Oh no, no," she says, smiling at me, the biscuits continuing to flop in perfect form on the pan. "This is my blessing in this life, Ashten darling."

Grandma Minnie once told me that she had a powerful realization one day when she was pregnant with Uncle Scott, her fourth child. She was working at the restaurant, raising the kids, doing the finances for both their house and the business and Grandpa John was never home but always here, working.

She told me that one day, she snapped when Grandpa John finally got home for dinner at nine o'clock that night after she'd made the kids wait until their dad got home to eat and everyone was crying. She told me that on that day, she'd realized that she would have to make a choice. She could see the things God had given her – the restaurant, her husband, her children – as blessings or as burdens.

"And sweetheart, therein lies the secret to happiness on this earth. You have a mortgage? Blessing, not burden. You have to do nine people's laundry while also working full time? Blessing – you have clothes to wear and a business that supports their purchase. You have to help your child through Algebra? Such a blessing because that child has the mental capacity to learn! Oh, Eliza! This is our blessing and happiness, my dear." And Grandma Minnie's eyes had shown with tears.

I watch Grandma Minnie now as she smiles at me and she pauses for half a second to pat my shoulder with her floured hand.

I have so much to learn. Sometimes I have this thought that maybe if I stay around Grandma Minnie enough, her character traits will sort of incubate into me, like catching the flu or something.

I pause by the counter to see if any of my orders are up and Will looks over at me. "Three minutes for Table 6."

"Thanks." I grab the full pitcher of freshly brewed coffee and head back out.

The word of the day is *confident*. I am going to look confident, I am going to act confident and I am going to think confident today.

I feel a little bit like Maria in *The Sound of Music*.

But if the Bible says we have confidence, then goodness, I will have confidence.

I stand up tall, I straighten my shoulders and I try to imagine myself looking like the pictures I've seen of my grandmother when she was thirty-one years old.

Granted, she had four kids by then, so she had to command a little bit of authority, but still.

I pour coffee, take out orders and I'm taking a five minute break to inhale a Dr. Pepper when Dad comes in, looking up to something.

"Ashten, good. Listen, I just sat a VIP in your section and I need you to make sure they are completely cared for at all times."

I nod. "Got it."

He watches me take a long drink of my Dr. Pepper and raises his eyebrows, pointing to the doorway. "Ashten! The VIP!"

"Right now?"

"Why not?"

"I just took my break."

"Breaks are only for salaried workers."

"What?" That's not true and Dad knows it.

Plus, I think it might be illegal.

I need to check that giant worker's rights poster by the cabinets in the back where all of us put our personal belongings when we get here. I think they have to hang the poster by law and I'm sure I remember seeing something about employees getting breaks.

Dad sighs at me and then rubs his head. "Look, Ashten, I know you just sat down, but the restaurant business waits for no man."

"Well, I guess it's lucky I am a woman then."

"Ashten."

"I'm going, I'm going." I down the rest of my drink and stand up, smoothing back out my apron and remembering my word of the day. I get my shoulders back, I take a deep breath and head out there, ready to see whatever movie star or politician or whoever Dad's idea of a VIP is.

I'd be more excited, but Dad one time told me a VIP was here and it was our mailman and not George Clooney, like I was hoping.

So, my hopes are pretty tempered.

I look around my section and every table is full, except for one table with just one person there and as soon as I make eye contact with them, I know exactly that I am looking right at Dad's VIP.

Oh Dad.

I walk over and pull out my notebook and pen.

Confident. I am confident.

"Hello, Mike," I say.

"Hey, Ashten."

"What can I get you to drink today?"

Mike is looking at me with his permanent frown face. A little kid two tables over is yelling shrilly and throwing his food, his parents are falling over themselves apologizing for everything.

Mike raises his eyebrows and slightly shakes his head at them, before turning that same expression to me.

"Little loud in here today," he says.

Confidence. I am full of confidence.

"We are usually pretty busy on the weekend," I tell him. "To drink?" I am purposefully light, cheerful and completely ignoring his tone.

Never mind that my back is cramping from all this tension running through my spine. I will be completely confident, even if it kills me.

The toddler is losing it, shrieking at the top of his lungs, the parents are basically groveling on the floor around me, an elderly man is yelling at his elderly wife to turn up her hearing aid so she can hear him and Mike is obviously about to snap.

"Can I speak with you outside?" he says and even though his sentence probably technically ends in a question mark, it is definitely not a question.

I have confidence. I have confidence.

Dear gracious, I have *confidence*.

I follow him through the insanely busy restaurant and out the front door, where there are at least four dozen people milling around on the giant front porch, rocking in the rocking chairs and taking selfies in front of the original Minnie's Diner sign that my grandfather hand carved for my grandmother when she first opened her shop thirty-five years ago.

Mike finally stops by one of the huge fruitless cherry trees and turns, squinting at me in the sun.

195

"Yes?" I ask, crossing my arms over my chest because I have this very bad feeling deep in my stomach. I am doing my best to be confident but the scowl on Mike's face isn't helping.

He takes a deep breath, lets it out and it sounds more like a growl than anything else. "Look. I don't know how to say this—"

Oh my gosh, something happened to Eliza.

All confidence is immediately gone and I am suddenly grabbing at his arm, feeling weak in my knees. "What's wrong? What happened? Is she okay?" My sentences are running together and I am immediately envisioning the hospital and oxygen masks and medically induced comas.

Mike looks at me. "What are you talking about?"

"Eliza. Is she okay?"

His frown deepens. "She is, unless you know something I don't know. Last I heard, she was taking a nap."

I inhale and step back, shaking my head. "Don't ever scare me like that again!" I say.

"I didn't say anything!"

"That was awful. I knew she had fallen asleep driving or the hospital had been taken hostage or something terrible."

Mike looks at me, opens his mouth, then just shakes his head and closes it again.

"What did you need to tell me?" I ask, trying to summon up the confidence again. But goodness, now that it's gone, I'm having a really hard time getting it back.

Especially because now my adrenaline is pumping like crazy and I'm trying to keep my hands from shaking. I cross my arms back over my chest.

Mike is still frown-squinting and he looks at me like he's trying to decide whether or not to actually talk. Finally, he half-shakes his head.

"Never mind," he says. "I'll talk to you about it another time."

Nice and cryptic.

"Okay," I say, because I was about ninety percent certain I didn't want to hear what he had to say anyway.

Call it women's intuition.

I turn to walk back inside and when I get to the door, I hold it open for him, but he's not behind me. And when I squint toward the parking lot, I can barely make out his white button-down shirt down one of the rows.

And apparently that was code for "goodbye".

Great. Maybe I can take my break now.

I check on all my tables, check on my orders and sit back down to the remaining three minutes of my break, this time with a sugar cookie.

See, this is why I will never be as thin as Katie or Eliza. They don't have desserts available constantly all day, every day throughout the entirety of swimsuit season.

Not that I have worn a swimsuit all season.

But still. It's the principal.

Dad comes in and he's got his hands spread and a "what happened" look on his face.

"What happened?" he asks.

Man, I totally nailed that look.

"I don't know," I say, wiping cookie crumbs off my shirt. "He asked to talk and then never did."

"Well, what did you say?"

"I didn't say anything."

Dad is worse than Katie and Eliza sometimes. Will calls a couple of my orders up and I shrug at Dad as I leave.

Mike does not help the whole confidence bit.

All day long, I see that annoyed frown on Mike's face and it takes everything in me to keep my shoulders straight.

I wish I saw him less. What happened to my grand plan of seeing him only at the wedding and then never again?

He seems so holier than thou. Which is not the easiest person to be around when you are attempting to feel some confidence in who you are.

Again, I don't get how he and Eliza are so close or even related at all.

198

Grandma Minnie touches my arm later that night as we are packing up to leave.

"You okay, honey? You seem a little down today."

It's just me and Grandma Minnie in the kitchen. Everyone else is gone or cleaning out front or already walking to their cars. Will left early to go look at flowers or tuxes or something wedding related with Everley.

There are so many weddings in my life right now. Everley hasn't asked me to be in hers, which part of me is a little relieved about.

More because I'm already having trouble juggling the two I'm in.

Grandma Minnie is waiting for me to respond and I know her. She will wait approximately seventeen years if that's what it takes for me to finally start talking.

I might as well tell her.

She must read my expression because she immediately takes off her coat and sits down at the little break table. She was carrying a to-go container and she pops it open, sliding the sugar cookies that didn't sell today in between us.

"Did you eat dinner?" she asks me when I sit down across from her.

I honestly can't remember if I ate or not.

She looks at me and stands, going into the giant closet fridge and coming out with all the makings for a deli sandwich. We make a few of them. My favorite is the Minnie Cristo. It's Grandma Minnie's homemade sweet white bread piled with honey roasted ham, Swiss cheese and a smidge of deli mustard, then it's battered in the beer batter, tossed in the deep fryer, sprinkled with powdered sugar and served with basically a bowl of her legendary raspberry sauce.

Grandma Minnie always told me that the raspberry is her favorite fruit and you can tell from the menu.

I've had people request bathtubs full of the sauce.

Needless to say, it's not a sandwich you could have every day. More like a once a year or at the most, every six to nine months. Otherwise, your arteries might commit suicide.

Grandma Minnie brings all the fixings over to the table and picks up a couple of paper towels. "So, go on, dear one. What's happening with you?"

I watch her cut four slices of homemade bread and I know she's sacrificing dinner with my grandpa to sit here and talk with me and my heart gets very warm. I love my grandmother. I can remember doing this so much growing up. I would come in during junior high and wash dishes or whatever and she would always take the time to talk to me and see what was going on. She's always had an open door and open ear policy with her grandchildren.

When you consider how many of us there are, that says a lot.

200

She spreads deli mustard on two of the slices, puts down Swiss and ham and then unscrews a jar and spreads a generous layer of the raspberry sauce on the other slices of bread, closing the two sandwiches. She smiles at me and slides one paper towel across the table. "I call this one 'The Fryer Is Already Clean Minnie Cristo'," she says and I grin.

"Probably better for me anyway."

"Oh, it's definitely better for the heart but maybe not for the soul," she says. "Let me pray. Jesus, be here with us, be with my Ashten and be with her heart. Let her know you and make you known. And bless our food. Amen."

"Amen," I say quietly.

Grandma Minnie takes a bite, swallows it and then nods to me. "Start talking."

"Well, Katie and Eliza are both engaged," I say.

Grandma Minnie nods. "I feel like I knew this."

"Right. And so, they are both so happy and I know that they mean well, and it's mostly Eliza, but she is constantly trying to set me up with her brother."

"How is her brother?"

I roll my eyes and Grandma Minnie smiles.

"Ah."

"He's not a nice person, Grandma. I mean, he seems nice when he's around Eliza, but he's super full of himself and kind of demeaning."

She nods. "Sounds like an unpleasant sort of person."

"Very unpleasant."

"Your father mentioned that a young man had come to
see you last week." She frowns, thinking. "And today? Or am
I separating the same event."

I sigh. "No. Daniel came last week. Mike, Eliza's
brother, was here today."

"Daniel, your old boyfriend?"

I don't know how Grandma Minnie remembers all this
stuff. I've mentioned how many of us there are. And I
guarantee she remembers just as much about all my
cousins.

I nod.

"Well, goodness, dear. All kinds of bees coming to
check out my flower."

"I just don't want to get stung."

She smiles at me. "I can understand that."

"I've been trying to be more confident," I tell her.

"I don't know why you would ever be anything but,"
she says. "You are lovely, you have a very respectable life
and Jesus loves you. Why would you ever feel unconfident?"

I think about Mike and his snort at the salad bar and
sigh. "Some people sometimes."

"Ashten."

"But it's okay. I've been reading in my devotions about
how we are supposed to be confident. Like what it says in
Hebrews 4."

Grandma Minnie is taking a bite of her sandwich, but she brightens right away. "Ah, you've been reading one of my very favorite chapters," she tells me after she swallows.

"Really?"

I love my grandmother. We've had many discussions about the Bible the entire time I was growing up and I'm pretty certain that every single verse or chapter or book I've ever brought up has been given the label of One of Her Favorites.

It makes me laugh.

"Oh yes," Grandma Minnie says. She quotes a different translation than my Bible, but it's the same exact verse. "'Let us then approach God's throne of grace with confidence, so that we may receive mercy and find grace to help us in our time of need.'"

Someday, I want to be like Grandma Minnie and be able to recall exact verses from memory at any given point of the day.

"That's exactly the one I've been studying," I tell her.

"It's a fantastic one to study," she says. "The 'throne of grace' is one of my favorite quotes in the whole Bible."

"I really like how it talks about being more confident. So I've been doing my best to try and have more."

Grandma Minnie looks at me, her head slightly tilted. "Have more what?" she asks me.

"Confidence. You know, I'm trying to have more confidence since that's what it says."

"Confidence in what?" Grandma Minnie asks. There's gentleness in her tone, nothing else.

"I guess the person who I am in Christ?"

Grandma Minnie thinks for a minute, finishes her sandwich and then pats my hand. "Sweetheart, I think you need to look more into the 'throne of grace' part of that verse. And I don't want any answers right now but I want you to do some thinking and praying about it. Sound good?"

I nod, finishing my sandwich, as well. Grandma Minnie squeezes my hand and smiles at me. "Let's go home, hmm? Early morning tomorrow and Grandpa will be worried about me."

"Okay, Grandma."

We clean up our dinner and I follow Grandma Minnie out, helping her lock the door and we walk the long walk across the parking lot to the employee spots.

"You should start parking closer to the building," I tell her, watching how slow her gait has become.

She waves a hand. "Please. This is the most exercise I get every day now. I used to walk miles before sunrise, to get some time alone with Jesus. Don't take away my only source of getting my heart rate up," she huffs.

I think I get so used to seeing Grandma Minnie and Grandpa John doing what they've always done that it's very shocking and terrifying to me to see them obviously aging.

There should be a rule that grandparents can become grandparents and then never get any older.

I drive home and Katie is in the living room, snuggled under one of her super thick blankets, watching *Call the Midwife.* The only thing I can see other than her head is her pink Minnie Mouse socks poking out from under the blanket.

"Hey!" she calls when I walk in.

"Hey." I stand behind the couch and watch the drama unfolding on the TV. I can't get into this show. Too much yuck. Eliza eats it up. She keeps saying that someday she's going to go get her midwifery license and start birthing babies.

I really want her to just birth her own babies so she doesn't do that. I feel like if, by some weird chance, I actually do find someone and get married, if Eliza became a midwife, I would have no other choice but to use her when that time came for me.

I watch the lady on the screen writhing in the pain of childbirth and I shake my head.

Nope. No ma'am. Epidurals were created for a reason.

The baby is born and snuggles into his tearful mother and Katie brushes away tears as the scene ends.

"Every time. Every time! I really need to start watching something else." She takes a deep breath, rubs her face and shakes her head. "Ah! Okay. So. How was your day, Ash?"

"Eh." I sit down on the other couch and immediately kick my shoes off, stretching out. Katie throws me the other blanket, which is super sweet but usually, I like to change out of my work clothes before I get too comfortable.

I shouldn't have sat down. The stale smells of the diner that have clung to my clothes are starting to gag me.

"I'll be right back." I run go change into some fleece pants I found on clearance last year and they are my favorite pants ever. They seriously feel like you're wearing straight fluff.

I pull on a sweatshirt and go out to the living room. Katie looks at me and grins.

"Do I need to turn the air off?"

"I mean, it is a little chilly in here."

Katie can be like a woman in the middle of menopause. She usually has our air set to sixty-five degrees in the day and it can get below sixty at night. She always tells me it's to hard to breathe if it gets above sixty-eight.

I don't even want to imagine how cold this house is going to be someday when she's pregnant or legitimately going through menopause. People will probably assume Olaf lives here.

I know she half keeps it that way so she can wear her cozy clothes and snuggle under blankets all year long though.

Katie peers over at the thermostat. "It's only sixty-two."

I lived in an apartment by myself for about six months of my life and I definitely kept it at least seventy-two degrees in there at all times.

Sometimes, I can't feel my fingers.

"So why was your day *eh*?" she asks me, pulling the blanket up around her neck.

I copy her position. "Well. We were packed all day so I didn't hardly get a break. And Mike came in on my one break I really had and Dad flipped out because I guess he asked to be seated in my section, but then he asked to talk to me and then didn't talk and left. And then Grandma Minnie stayed late with me and talked to me about some of the stuff I've been reading in the Bible and made me a sandwich and that was nice. So at least the day ended well."

Katie is nodding through my whole speech. Katie is a good listener.

"So, Mike came?"

I knew that was going to be the first thing she said to me. "Yeah." I lean my head back and sigh at the ceiling. "He was acting all frowny and weird too. Though, he's always frowny so I guess that part wasn't weird."

"He's not always frowning. I've seen him smile."

"I have too. A couple of times. I think." I think he smiled more than once during my impromptu breakfast with him and Eliza the other day.

It's such a pity because he really has a nice smile.

"No more news from Daniel?" Katie asks. "And on that note, do you feel like Aretha Franklin?"

For the life of me, I cannot figure out the connection between Daniel and me being Aretha Franklin. Did she live in Alaska? Did her boyfriend leave her to go to Alaska too? Was she dating someone named Daniel?

I look at Katie. "Okay, you're going to have to help me out here, but to answer your question, no, I don't feel like her. I'm not sure I've ever felt like Aretha Franklin, though I'd love to have her voice. And her success wouldn't be too terrible either."

Katie grins. "Didn't she sing 'It's Raining Men'?" She pulls her phone over and started typing and makes a little *hmph* sound a second later. "What do you know. She didn't. Could've sworn that was her."

"Well. Anyway, it's not raining men."

"Daniel, Mike, Dillon. I've been hearing a lot of men's names in the same sentence with yours lately."

I scrunch my eyebrows together. "Who is Dillon?"

"I don't know. Eliza said something about you and Dillon."

"I don't think I even know anyone named Dillon."
Then I roll my eyes. "Wait, Eliza said this? I think she meant
Daniel." She will never get his name right.

I will end up marrying this guy and she will know him
all of our lives and someday our children will marry each
other and she'll give a mother of the bride speech at the
wedding and will end up thanking me and Drake or Dominic
or Diego for our help with the day.

Katie grins. "Okay, so it's raining a couple of men."

"I'm not sure two is considered a rainstorm. And one
of them isn't interested."

"Daniel?"

"Mike."

Katie snorts and it's exactly the same snort that Mike
gave that waiter at the salad bar.

"I *hate* when people do that."

"Sorry. I think you're ridiculous."

"Yeah, well, I'm not. That's partly what Grandma
Minnie and I were talking about tonight too."

"You being ridiculous?"

"No, trying to be confident in who I am."

Katie looks at me for a long moment, so long, that I
start getting a little squirrely. It's like she's reading my soul.

I chicken out. "Well, I'm exhausted and we've got
church tomorrow."

I think Katie knows I don't want to talk about it so she finally nods. "Sweet dreams, Ash."

"Night Katie."

I brush my teeth, pull on my pajamas, attempt and finally give up trying to untangle my hair, wash my face and climb into bed. I look at my Bible and turn the light off.

The throne of grace.

I mean, wasn't that just another word for heaven? I'm not exactly sure what Grandma Minnie wants me to be thinking about.

CHAPTER *Thirteen*

Our church is possibly one of the most "Come As You Are" churches I've ever been to, but it never fails that every week, I stand in front of my closet in my robe, totally blanking on what to wear.

Do I wear a skirt and be "fancy" for church? Do I wear jeans and be casual? Do I risk the wrath of Grandma Minnie, even though she doesn't go to my church, and wear leggings and a tunic?

I immediately shake my head at the last one. She may be firmly rooted in First Baptist Carrington Springs for like the last sixty years, but the day I dare to wear leggings to church will hands down be the day Grandma Minnie and Grandpa John decide to come check out the new church little Ashten is going to and I will never hear the end of it.

Never mind that there's a part of my soul that is terrified that if I wear those to church, it will be the unforgiveable sin.

Grandma Minnie *really* hates leggings.

I half-growl at the closet and reach for a pair of my skinny jeans and a short-sleeved, white shirt. I'll put on my blue canvas flats and pretend I'm being patriotic today.

I cuff up the bottom of my jeans and go put on some makeup.

Katie is finishing up breakfast by the time I get out there.

"Hey."

"Morning," she smiles at me. "Sleep well?"

"Eh." Not really.

I don't know what Grandma Minnie wants me to think about and it's bugging me. She's not usually so cryptic.

Katie gives me a look but Eliza walks in right then and distracts her. "Hey, Katie?" she asks as soon as she opens the door.

"No."

"I didn't even ask the question yet!"

"Are you wanting to borrow some of my clothes?"

Eliza gapes at her. "When have I ever asked to borrow your clothes?"

"Um, last week. And two weeks before that. And I still haven't gotten either of those shirts back."

"I have nothing to wear."

"You have millions of cute clothes."

"They are all dirty from work."

"You wear scrubs to work!" Katie rolls her eyes.

"Exactly," Eliza grins.

"No," Katie says again. "You'd better get ready quick. We are leaving in five minutes."

It is seriously this same scene every single week.

Come November, I'm curious what will happen. Will all four of them just get in the same car and go together? Or will Katie leave Luke since he will probably still be in bed?

Part of me wants to find a realtor to show me houses in this neighborhood so I can catch the drama every week. I could start going to a later service, go sit on my front porch with my cereal and watch. It would be like my own personal neighborhood reality TV show.

Honestly, back in the days before TV, I think this is what most people did on their front porches.

We get to church and Eliza is actually wearing a shirt that she purchased herself. Katie puts the car in park and Eliza leans up to the front seat. "Guys, could you be praying for us? Cooper is going to talk to his boss tomorrow about potentially either working from home here in Carrington Springs or opening up a satellite office here. I think we've decided that we will live here. Mike's here, I love my job and I own a house and Cooper is still in an apartment."

I am nodding through most of her speech. I was really hoping they would stay here.

Katie immediately reaches back and gives Eliza possibly the most awkward car hug ever. "I'm so glad you are going to stay," she says.

Eliza grins. "Me too."

"I was trying to be supportive either way, but I've already been praying for you to stay here. I'll keep praying for Cooper's job."

"Me too," I tell her. For the life of me, I cannot remember what Cooper does for a living, but hopefully it's something he can do here.

"Let's get inside," Katie says, looking at her watch.

I smile.

Katie plops her Bible on the aisle seat and sits down next to it. Eliza sits next to her and I scoot down one so Mike can sit by her.

No way am I starting what happened last week all over again.

I half consider switching to a completely different aisle, but Katie and Eliza would lose their minds.

Already, they are both looking at me weird.

"What?" I ask, pulling out my chapstick.

"I did take a shower this morning," Eliza says. She sniffs her underarm. "And I am like ninety-seven percent sure I put on deodorant."

Katie laughs. "Only ninety-seven percent?"

"Well, I worked all night and so I was kind of going through the motions this morning."

"I still don't see how you do it," Katie says.

"You get used to it. Anyway. What gives, Ash?"

I shake my head. "This way, it's not all weird when—"

"Hey."

Mike is squeezing down the aisle then and he sees the spot next to Eliza and sits down.

There. Plan worked. Probably during the music, I could sort of inch my way over and end up with a seat between us.

Mike looks over and gives me this sort of pained half-smile, like he's sitting on something uncomfortable or he's not sure what to say.

I mean, "Good morning," isn't too difficult.

It's nice and weird.

"Hi," I say.

"Hi."

Then we both sit there avoiding eye contact like awkward birds on a phone wire.

Though, birds' eyes are on the sides of their heads, so maybe when they are all sitting in a row with their heads all facing forward, they are really sitting there looking at each other.

Too deep of thought for a Sunday early morning.

The music starts and Luke is nowhere to be seen, per usual. I start inching my way down the aisle a touch.

Plan is in progress and appears to be working successfully. Two more songs and if I move an inch every thirty seconds, I can be in the next chair over before our associate pastor comes up to give the announcements.

215

Someone is suddenly standing next to me on the right and I look over and Daniel has somehow materialized there.

"Morning," he whispers, all conspiratorially like we are the best of friends and I saved him that empty seat.

Um, I did not, thank you very much. And did I mention that I changed churches and come here now? How did he find me?

This whole thing is weird.

And now Mike is looking at me and then Daniel and his mouth is in this straight line and he's not even pretending to sing.

Great. Somehow my not inviting my ex-boyfriend to church has also offended him.

All these people who advocate for small towns have no idea what they are talking about. I need to move. To like the biggest city in the world.

Maybe New York.

I went to New York with Katie and Eliza once. It was pretty dirty. And the cab ride almost killed us. But the cinnamon roll I got at this little corner bakery was good. I could maybe live there.

At least then I could sort of put my headphones on and blend in with the crowd, all *Win A Date with Tad Hamilton* style.

Or maybe that was in Los Angeles.

It's been awhile since I've seen that movie.

216

I should watch that movie.

Tad Hamilton might not have been the world's best guy but he was at least semi-sweet.

Like a chocolate chip.

I close my eyes and try to remind myself that I am at church and this is supposed to be a worship service. Not a figure out some random movie while trying to avoid thinking of the two people on either side of me time.

Daniel lightly elbows me in the arm. "So, this music is nice," he whispers.

I really want to burst into that line from the Gwyneth Paltrow movie version of *Emma* and be all, "KINDLY REFRAIN FROM THE INTIMACY OF WHISPERING", but I kind of smash my lips together and raise my eyebrows at him like, "Yep! It is!" but I don't say anything back.

Meanwhile, Mike is obviously stewing next to me and I don't even know what I did or if it's even about me. Maybe he hates this song.

It's not my favorite song either but at least I'm pretending to sing.

Kind of.

The lead guitar guy starts into another praise chorus and it's all I can do to not pretend nature is calling and run for my car.

Dear gracious, how many songs are we going to sing?

Although, it will be worse when we are done. Then I'll have to sit still in between the two guys for the entire sermon. And Pastor Mark, for all his strong points, does not preach short sermons.

Which was part of the reason I liked him in the first place, but today, it is a quality I hate.

Maybe I can slide out to use the restroom and then say it was going to be too disruptive to come back to our row and I can sit in the back.

Yes.

This could work.

I am about to slide out when the associate pastor comes on stage and starts to pray.

Man.

"Go ahead and take a seat," he says when he finishes.

And there goes my chance.

We all sit and my one mission in life is to avoid eye contact with any person on my row. Which is difficult, because Luke sneaks into the aisle then, looks down the row at all of us and then just grins this big old grin and gives me an obnoxious thumbs up.

If we weren't in church and the whole building wasn't quietly listening to the last of the announcements, he would totally be all *you go, girl* to me.

Luke is nothing if not annoying.

I have a two handed grip on my Bible, my feet are flat on the floor, my back is ramrod straight. I am already feeling tension in my upper back but no way am I leaning back against the seat or crossing my legs one way or the other.

Not after what Cher says in *Clueless* about it being some sort of invitation.

Jesus. Please let this be the week that Pastor Mark loses his voice and we are all dismissed early. You could do that, Lord. I know You could.

Maybe it's pretty un-Christian of me to be praying for my own pastor to lose his voice, but I see no other way around this, other than the people behind me to spontaneously combust or vomit or discover that they have been bitten by a radioactive spider or something and it puts the whole church into an uproar.

Or maybe, today, right now, is when the rapture is supposed to happen.

Yes, Lord. Rapture now. That would be fantastic.

I am getting sticks and straw in my heavenly crown right now.

Pastor Mark comes on stage and smiles at all of us. "Friends, today is a good day," he says and everyone all murmurs their consent, like they do every week.

Except for me. I do not murmur. And neither does Mike. Daniel kind of bobs his head and smiles.

He is mistaken.

Today is not a good day.

Somehow, I make it through the sermon. I don't think I hear a single word. I opened my Bible, I nodded occasionally, I smiled tightly at the comic relief Pastor Mark would say, but I could not tell you what passage we read or what he said.

Not one word. I can't remember one word and Pastor Mark barely left the stage.

The guitar player is back and he's asking everyone to stand and my back is so locked tight from the tension that I can barely unfold out of the chair. I look older than my grandmother trying to stand up.

Mike shoots me a look out of the corner of his eye and as I grab for the chair in front of me and Daniel acts all concerned but I roll my shoulder and wave him off.

You don't get the ability to pretend to care about me if you're going to up and leave when we are dating.

Daniel and the rest of the congregation sing another song while Mike and I stand there all stiffly and he's gone before the last sounds of the guitar have even faded out of the church.

Daniel, meanwhile, is chattering about how great the music was and how convicting the sermon was and he could totally see why I switched to this church. And Eliza, Katie and Luke are looking at me and then to Daniel and back and me and finally, Luke kind of pushes around Katie and holds his hand out to Daniel.

"Hey. I'm Luke."

"Daniel. Nice to meet you."

"And how do you know Ashten?"

"She's an old friend," Daniel says and he has this tender look in his eyes. If it were on anyone else, it might make my heart squeeze a little bit.

But it's on him. So all it does is make my defenses go even higher.

At this point, me and my defenses are going to have trouble getting back through the doorways.

"Anyone up for lunch?" Daniel asks all casually, but I can totally read between the lines and know he's trying to get back onto the good side of me by infiltrating my friends.

Eliza and Katie exchange a look and then they both look at me and must see the panic because they both start shaking their heads.

Eliza talks first. "Ah, sorry. I worked all night. I'm a nurse so I need to go home and take a nap. But thanks for the offer."

"Yeah, and actually, Ashten and I were already planning on doing some wedding stuff. Luke and I are getting married in a couple of months."

Apparently, I am doing wedding stuff today.

Best news I've heard all day.

Daniel nods. "All right, well maybe next time."

"Mm," Katie says all noncommittally and then she looks at her phone and gasps at the time. "Oh my goodness, we need to go. Nice to meet you, Daniel."

We all walk outside and I sort of wave all awkwardly and climb into the back of Katie's car.

Where I immediately fall over across the backseat and pull my legs into the fetal position, moaning.

Eliza gets in, cackling like a wicked old witch, spreading cookie crumbs around the town.

Katie looks back at me in the rear view mirror, starting the car and grinning. "Poor Ashten."

Eliza is still laughing. "I've never seen people sit so straight and not move even once. Y'all looked like a painting. I mean, if Pastor Mark had gone any longer, I swear to you that both Ashten and Mike would have sort of went *zert!* and stayed like that forever. We would have had to pick you up and move you to some kind of museum, like that wax thing in Vegas or something."

I moan.

"Poor Ashten," Katie says again, but she's still smiling.

"Why, why, why, why?" I'm still moaning but at least it's now in English.

Eliza smirks. "Sermon was good though. Timely for you, considering all these hoards of men attempting to woo you."

222

"I didn't hear one word."

"That's a shame. It was all about how we should boast in Christ and not in ourselves. And how we can be confident that God has a plan for us and He is going to make the way sure."

I sit up, rubbing my head. "Sounds like it would have been a good one."

"It was. Possibly one of his best."

"Put your seatbelt on," Katie tells me in the mirror. "I'm waiting to leave."

I click my belt and she starts driving back to the house.

"So that was Daniel," Eliza says.

"That was Daniel."

"He's kind of cute." The way she says it though is a little like when you give someone a food they hate and they're all like, "Yeah, it was great," like they are trying to convince themselves that they liked it too.

"Sorry, I don't see it." At least Katie is honest.

"Me either. I was just being nice."

And it looks like they are both adopting the honest approach.

I shake my head. "He didn't have the long hair before."

"I mean, it would look better short, but still. I don't see it."

"You guys both prefer clean cut."

223

"You don't?" Eliza asks.

"I don't know if I have a preference."

"Come on, Ash. Everyone has a type."

"I hate that word."

"Type?"

"Yeah. I honestly don't think that everyone has a type. So maybe I'm more attracted to someone and not someone else, but that doesn't mean that I'm only attracted to people like the first one. I could be attracted to others too."

Eliza looks back at me, frowning. "Sorry, you lost me after the second attraction."

"I've known people who have a definite type," Katie says. "One girl I worked with only dated men named Charles."

"I don't even think I know a man named Charles," Eliza says.

"You would be out of luck then."

"Doomed to singleness forever. Oh well. I keep myself plenty entertained."

I smile.

We get to the house.

"And I don't have a hoard of men wooing me," I say, climbing out of the car.

"You have at least two."

"Two is not a 'hoard'. And even that is debatable."

Eliza nods. "I know. We *are* debating right now. I say two can be a hoard. I mean, think about it, if you were standing there and two men started to run right at you, would you move? Yes. Would you move if there was a hoard of men running right at you? Yes. Therefore, two men is equal to a hoard of men. Trust me. I was really good at those type of questions in geometry."

I sigh. "I *meant* that it was debatable that there are even two men interested. Not whether or not they are concerned a hoard or even equal to one."

"Oh. Well, be like butter next time and clarify."

Katie is dying.

I am in the process of rubbing off any makeup I applied to my face and possibly some of my epidermis.

"I still think you need to give Mike a chance," Eliza says.

"Look, can we make a rule that we don't discuss things about your brother? It's just weird."

Eliza looks at Katie. "Do you think it's weird?"

"A little," she nods to Eliza. "More weird for you than me."

"Well, it's not weird for me. I know Mike the best and I also know his flaws the best. And trust me, he has flaws."

I am immediately hearing that line Michael Scott says on *The Office* playing in my head.

"Guess what, I have flaws. What are they? Oh, I don't know. I sing in the shower. Sometimes I spend too much time volunteering. Occasionally I'll hit somebody with my car."

Now I am trying my best to hold it together because it's not really an appropriate time to laugh.

Eliza is still talking. "He can be super annoying. And over-protective and he does not like change."

"Does he sing in the shower?" Katie asks, straight-faced.

I snort.

Eliza looks at the both of us and shakes her head.

"I bet he spends too much time volunteering," Katie continues.

I am hard core giggling now.

"Maybe he, I don't know, occasionally hits someone with his car."

Eliza rolls her eyes and starts walking across the street to her house. "I am going to bed. Y'all laugh now, but watch, I am totally right about everything!"

I laugh.

CHAPTER *Fourteen*

Monday mornings are always the slowest at Minnie's Diner. Mostly because we are all still tired from being up debating with the uncles and trying to solve the world's problems with the aunts at Grandma Minnie and Grandpa John's house the night before.

It makes for a long day, if you're scheduled for the long shift on Monday.

Which I am.

I yawn and go exchange my empty coffee pot for the full one in the back and check on my orders. Everyone is dragging in the back.

I was the first one to leave my grandparents' house last night and I didn't leave until almost ten.

No wonder we are all sloth-like today.

I walk out to my half-full section and start making the coffee round again. Michelle, my cousin who was scheduled to do hostessing today, is sitting a new table in my section, so I hold the coffee pot in my right hand and dig my pad out with my left, because odds are good at nine in the morning, the customers are going to want coffee. I might as well keep the pot with me.

I suddenly have an incredible case of déjà vu.

Mike is sitting at the table, alone again, in the corner booth.

I mean, does he request that specific booth?

I take a deep breath and walk over and I can feel the tightness in my spine again. I think my back is remembering the stiffness from the last time I was around him yesterday.

"Hi," I say, walking over.

"Hello."

"Would you like some coffee?"

"Please." He slides over an empty cup. We set the tables with the silverware, water glasses and coffee cups. Saves us a couple of steps.

I pour the coffee and try to think about confidence so my hand will stop wanting to shake.

It's not working well.

I set the coffee pot on the table and clear my throat, holding my pad and pencil. "Have you decided what you would you like to eat?"

"Can we talk?"

And now the déjà vu is full blown.

Here we go again. I take a deep breath and shrug. "Sure."

"Outside?"

"Why not?"

I follow him outside and he stops by the very same tree as the last time.

Honestly, I'm not really expecting him to say anything. We are going to most likely have a repeat of last week and I will go back inside in a few minutes.

Which will be the best option for my hair, anyway.

I'm hoping this doesn't become our new thing. He comes, takes up the corner booth, doesn't order anything, we go outside, he doesn't say anything and then he leaves and I miss out on a tip.

Mike has frown line so deep between his eyes, I'm worried that a little bird is going to think it's a safe place to set up a nice nest for the fall.

"Are you seeing that guy?"

I really want to reply that the only guy I am presently seeing is him, because he's right in front of me, but I bite back the sarcasm. "What guy?"

"Beard. Shaggy."

"Daniel?"

"Sure."

"No."

"Does he know you aren't seeing him?"

Again, I bite the sarcasm back. "Yes."

"Are you sure?"

Now I'm confused. "Am I sure that I'm not seeing him?"

"Yes."

His one word, sharp answer does not help the confusion.

"What are you asking me?" I finally say.

"Look, Ashten, I find you..." he lets his voice drag off, huffing and he rubs his forehead, raking a hand back through his hair.

Mike is a nice enough looking person but he's obviously not doing too well today. He looks haggard.

I wait for him to finish, but if he takes too much longer, I'm going to have to let him figure it out while I go take orders out before Will fires me. Grandma Minnie might not have the heart to do it, but Will wouldn't even blink twice.

"Are you okay?" I ask him, which is a dumb question, because he's obviously not.

"Look, despite everything, I like you. Okay? So I was thinking maybe we could figure out a time to go get coffee or something."

I look at him. "What?"

He huffs his breath out again. "This was not a good idea. I'm sorry for bothering you." Then he turns and walks across the parking lot, climbing into his truck.

I go back inside and I'm picking up my tray full of orders and avoiding Will's frustrated glare before I really think about what Mike just said.

Despite everything, he likes me.

Despite what, exactly?

Who even says that?

"Oh. My. Gosh." Katie's mouth is open like one of those sucker fish at the aquarium and her voice sounds exactly like Chandler's girlfriend on *Friends*. She's standing over a crockpot shredding what smells like some sort of chicken with lime.

"Okay, simmer down, Janice."

I got home a few minutes ago and I'm not in the mood. I've been stewing on what Mike said all day long and now I'm mad.

Despite everything.

You know what? I am a pretty likable person, thank you very much. I am, for the most part, a normal person with normal habits and normal facial expressions.

He can't even say that.

Mr. Grumpus.

"No, Ashten!" She runs to the sink, rinses the chicken off her hands and sprints for the TV. "Look!"

She queues up *Pride and Prejudice* and we are at the scene where Mr. Darcy is first attempting to tell Elizabeth that he loves her.

"You must allow me to tell you how ardently I admire and...love you."

It's sweet and adorable, if not awkward. It's in no way shape or form any resemblance to what just happened to me.

Maybe the awkwardness, but sweet and adorable awkward is way different than horrific and insulting awkward.

"Katie."

"Ashten!" Katie is gesturing to the TV like she is about to start a career flipping letters after people spin a giant wheel. "It's the same thing!"

"It most definitely is *not*, thank you."

"He told her he loved her and then he insulted her! Mike insulted you and then told you he likes you! It's a little bit reversed, but it's the same thing!"

I leave and go back in the kitchen, but Katie follows me.

I need something to eat. I start digging through the pantry, because I know we surely have something.

"I'm making chicken tacos."

"I need chocolate."

Katie is all giggly. "You like him!"

I yank my head out of the pantry. "How is me needing chocolate synonymous with me liking him?"

"Girl, everyone knows that."

"Okay, well, I do not like him."

"Why not?"

I step away from the pantry and start checking the points off on my fingers. I've had all day to figure out how much I do not like this man.

"He's arrogant. He's conceited. He's overbearing."

"Pretty sure all of those are the same thing, but go ahead," Katie interrupts, back to shredding chicken.

"He is not kind to anyone, except for Eliza."

"Not necessarily a bad trait, but continue."

"He's selfish, he's moody, he's annoying and he's generally, not a nice person to be around."

Katie smiles at me. "That's quite the list you've got there."

"You know how people are always like, 'I knew he was the right one because of the person he brings out in me'?"

She nods all slowly. "I think so."

"Like, you and Luke. Luke brings out a really fun side of you that a lot of people don't get to see."

"So I'm not fun unless Luke is around?"

I growl out a sigh and Katie grins.

"You are so difficult."

"Hey, this is Mike we are insulting, not me. Don't get confused here. Sheesh. Moody. Look at the pot calling the kettle black."

"I'm just saying, if anything, Mike brings out the worst in me and that is not a trait that I like."

"Okay, okay," Katie says. "So what did you say after he told you he liked you?"

"I did get the chance to say anything. He started saying this was a bad idea and he stomped across the parking lot and left."

"Aw," Katie says, tipping her head to the side.

"No, Katie."

"What? I am allowed to think it's kind of cute."

"It was not cute. It was awful. We need to work on your definition of cute because your definition is wrong."

"Again, let's remember who we are insulting here."

Eliza pops her head in the door then and inhales. "I thought I smelled chicken and heard yelling. The sights and smells of home. It's like a Hallmark movie."

I immediately look at Katie. "Not a word," I hiss.

"Not a word about what?" Eliza closes the door behind her and comes over, pulling out a barstool and sitting down, looking at me and then at Katie.

Katie gives me a look. "It appears that I am not allowed to say. I will add *bossy* to my list for Ashten."

"Oo, are we making lists? What's mine?" Eliza is grinning, reaching for a bite of chicken and Katie smacks her hand.

"I'm sorry, are your hands clean?"

"I just washed them!"

"Since you touched the door handle?"

Eliza rolls her eyes. "Sheesh. Germaphobe. There's another for your list."

"You work at a hospital! You're a nurse! You're supposed to know these things!"

"I wash my hands before I leave the hospital," Eliza says, grumpily going over and scrubbing her hands in the sink. "Why are we making lists?"

Katie opens her mouth and I glare at her.

"Oh come on," Eliza says, rolling her eyes and sitting back down after she dries her hands off. "You know I'm going to find out eventually. You might as well tell me now."

"I mean, she is pretty persistent," Katie says to me. "We can put it on her list. But you might as well tell her."

"She's a meddler."

"Hello! I am sitting right here," Eliza says, grinning. She reaches for a bite of chicken and Katie smacks her hand again. "What? I washed! You watched me wash!"

"We are eating in ten minutes, you can wait."

"So I washed for nothing?"

"You washed so I won't catch whatever is at the hospital. Scurvy or something."

Eliza rolls her eyes. "You'll be pleased to know that I haven't had a patient with scurvy yet this week, so I'm thinking you might be safe."

I know Eliza is going to find out, though I don't think Mike will tell her, at least of his own free will. And maybe not even in the near future.

But she will find out.

I guess I might as well get it over with.

"Fine." I sit down on the barstool next to Eliza and cover my face with my hands.

"What happened?" Eliza asks. "Did Dale show up again?"

I moan.

Katie laughs. "I think it's Daniel, friend. And no. He didn't. But someone else did."

By the silence and then the elation, I can tell Eliza puts two and two together and she's immediately up, jumping around the kitchen and then grabbing my hands, yanking them away from my face. "WE ARE GOING TO BE SISTERS!"

"Oh no, we aren't." I have to basically yell to be heard over her celebration and she immediately freezes and then frowns at me, still holding my hands.

My goodness, she looks just like her brother when she frowns.

"Well, why not?"

"Because, *despite everything*, I still don't like him."

Katie starts laughing and Eliza looks confused.

"He told her that despite everything, he liked her," Katie says.

Eliza's expression doesn't change for a minute, then she goes all guppy-like the same way Katie did. "Oh. My. Gosh."

"Oh, come on. Not you, too. Seriously?" I ask, as Eliza drops my hands to cup them over her own mouth.

"He *said* that?" Her eyes are huge, she's looking at Katie, who is nodding with equal enthusiasm.

"I know."

"That's exactly like what—"

"I know."

"I mean, it's obviously a little more modern day—"

"I know."

"But it's like he's—"

"Mr. Darcy!" The two of them say it together and Katie is still nodding.

"I know," she says again.

Meanwhile, I am back on the barstool and I think my head has started shaking on its own.

"How can you not see this?" Eliza gasps at me.

"Because, it's not the same. At all."

She is not listening. "I guess this makes me Georgiana." She grins. "I always liked her. I'll need to learn how to play the piano."

Katie laughs.

I climb into bed later that night, after rehashing the story so many times that I'm starting to think it maybe didn't even happen.

Katie and Eliza are still in shock that I actually said no.

But I didn't even say no. I don't remember saying anything other than maybe asking him what he was talking about at first.

Still.

Despite everything.

There's this pit in my stomach and I pull over my Bible, flipping it open to Hebrews. I'm going to have a permanent crease here if I'm not careful.

I read back through the verses again, trying to do anything to take my mind off those two words that Mike said earlier.

Therefore, since we have a great high priest who has passed through the heavens, Jesus the Son of God, let us hold fast our confession. For we do not have a high priest who cannot sympathize with our weaknesses, but One who has been tempted in all things as we are, yet without sin. Therefore let us draw near with confidence to the throne of grace, so that we may receive mercy and find grace to help in time of need.

I look at verse fifteen again. *We do not have a high priest who cannot sympathize with our weaknesses, but One who has been tempted in all things as we are.*

Maybe…

Maybe this is what Grandma Minnie was trying to hint at. Jesus sits on a throne of grace and our confidence has very little to do with ourselves and what we think we can handle, even with Jesus' help.

Our confidence comes from knowing that He has been here.

He's felt rejection.

He's felt unworthy.

But He did not sin. Instead, He is now in heaven, on His throne and has nothing but grace for us.

So we can confidently go to Him, knowing that He knows.

I look at the verses and it's like I'm reading them for the first time.

I close the Bible, turn the light off and just lay there in the darkness for a long time.

Let us approach the throne of grace with confidence.

Despite everything…

CHAPTER *Fifteen*

I am not a fun person to be around the next morning at 6AM.

Grandma Minnie finally stops me as I stomp past, calling me over while she rolls out piecrusts.

"Are you okay, Ashten darling?"

Based on the way she's looking at me, I think she knows the answer to her non-question.

I sigh and set down the coffee pot on the long work table she's at.

"Why don't you pull up a chair," she says, nodding to one of the counter-height chairs that we have scattered around the table.

Ideally, they are for Grandma Minnie and Grandpa John to use while they are here working, but they are rarely ever sitting.

"What's going on, honey?"

I look at Grandma. "Well. I need grace."

"We all do," she nods.

"With a certain person."

She smiles. "I see. Is it your brother?"

"No."

240

"Your father?"

"No."

"Must be one of those men who keeps coming in here requesting to be sat in your section then." Grandma Minnie is smirking now.

"It's not funny."

"It's a little funny, sweetheart. And honestly, it's way past time. What did he do?"

"He told me that 'despite everything', he liked me."

She looks at me. "And?"

"And what?"

"What did you say?"

"Grandma, that was so insulting!"

She rolls out another circle of the dough and then looks at me again. "Maybe I didn't hear you correctly," she says. "He said despite everything, he liked you."

"Right."

"And this makes you upset."

She is not following this, apparently. "'Despite everything', Grandma. He basically said, 'Even though you're awful, I guess I still like you'."

"But he didn't say that."

"He basically did."

"But he didn't though."

"He used other words."

Grandma half-laughs at me and it only makes me more mad, but I am trying my best to shove it down.

"Oh Ashten. Your generation makes me laugh."

"It's not funny," I say again.

"Sweetheart, I'm not laughing at you." She pauses and then shrugs. "Okay, I'm kind of laughing at you. But honey, you need to remember that in my generation, we didn't beat around the bush like you young people do today. There wasn't this constant worry about feelings and we didn't bruise so easily."

She lays the piecrusts into the aluminum pans while she talks and then pulls over the giant bowl of pears that have been resting in a mixture of sugar, cinnamon, a few dashes of cloves and vanilla.

"When your grandfather first asked me out, he told me that he'd never thought he would ask a girl with such shabby clothes to a dance."

"Grandpa said that?" I am aghast. Grandpa John is the sweetest man I've ever met.

Grandma Minnie grins. "Like I said, we didn't bruise as easily. My clothes *were* shabby. I didn't come from a very wealthy family. And Grandpa's family was definitely more well off. His father was a doctor and they had more than we did. It wasn't a bad thing, it just was."

She scoops the pear mixture into the piecrusts and smiles over at me. "I'm not saying that you should go out

242

with this man, perhaps he is a terrible person and you should stay away. I'm only saying, don't jump to conclusions and don't lay down the cross of Christ to pick up the burden of offense."

Will calls one of my orders up and Grandma Minnie nods to me, smiling. "You'd better go, my dear."

I stand, put the coffee pot back and carry out my order to the waiting family.

Grandma Minnie's words bug me the rest of the morning.

Don't lay down the cross of Christ to pick up the burden of offense.

I get home about five, the dinner crowd was slow and Will sent several of us home early. Tuesday nights are never busy at the restaurant.

Eliza is sitting on our couch, wearing a beat up pair of jeans and a paint-spotted sweatshirt. Her hair is falling out of a messy bun and she's wearing glasses.

"Hey," she grins at me when I walk in.

"Hi. Off today?"

"You know it."

"Where's Katie?"

"I think I was bugging her so she went to Panera."

"Why aren't you at your house?"

"Because I knew you would miss me if I wasn't here."

I half laugh. This is totally Eliza.

I plop down on the other couch and lean my head back against the cushions.

"So."

I know exactly what she's going to ask me, so I don't even move. "Mm."

"Mike."

"Leave it alone, Eliza."

"Is it so bad that I want you guys to be happy?"

"And who better to care for our happiness than you, right?"

"See? Now you are getting it." She grins at me and then sobers. "I think you haven't seen the real Mike yet."

"So who have I been seeing? The fake Mike?"

"He's one of those people who takes awhile to let people in."

"Mm-hmm."

"Really. And I think it has a lot to do with my parents. He never was like this until after Dad died. And then when Mom died too, he became very closed off to most people. The fact that he told you he liked you in the first place is so out of his comfort zone."

I rub my forehead.

"Plus, I think if you didn't like him at least a little bit, it wouldn't be bothering you this much."

"I'm not bothered." It's such a lie.

Eliza rolls her eyes. "Please. It's me. You don't have to lie."

I really don't think I like Mike.

Sometimes, I honestly can't even stand him.

I'm sure he's a nice enough person, maybe. I doubt he kicks dogs or purposefully smashes snails on the sidewalks or refuses to help little old ladies get canned green beans off of the top shelves in grocery stores.

And he's nice enough looking, I guess. He's not tall, he's not short, he's sort of average. And he's not skinny and he's not large. He's again, average. His hair is shorter than Daniel's but longer than a buzz cut. He's not movie star attractive, but he's cute in a normal person kind of a way.

Eliza is looking at me. "So, what's the hold up?"

"Honestly?"

"Honestly."

"He's insulting."

"How so?"

"He snorts."

"Like a pig?"

"Exactly. And then there's the whole 'despite everything' line."

"Maybe you need him to explain that one to you."

"Use the butter line?"

"What?"

"You know, the one you told me the other day about clarifying."

She grins. "Oh yeah. That is a great line."

I smile at her and then shake my head. "I don't know, Eliza. I think if it were meant to be, it would be easier than this."

"I'm sorry, where do you find that in the Bible?"

"What?"

"That we were meant to have an easy life."

"I'm not saying that we were meant to have an easy life, but look at you and Cooper. All of us could see that you guys were meant to end up together. You guys have so much chemistry, you could start your own lab somewhere."

She laughs. "Yeah, well, that wasn't always the case."

"Anyway. I want to have that too. You know? Spark. And I don't think it's there."

"Aren't you the one who was telling Katie that it wasn't that big of a deal?"

I think back to before Katie and Luke were dating and nod slightly. "Maybe."

"I'm going to tell you something my mama wrote for me," Eliza says and her eyes and tone get all soft like they always do when she talks of her mother. "'Don't toss aside the diamond in the rough for the polished and shiny rhinestone.'"

"Which means what? Don't accept anything less than a carat?"

She snorts and goodness, she sounds just like her brother.

"No, it means, don't do what I do and always think there's something better out there."

"Do you think there's something better out there than Cooper?"

"Not anymore, but I used to. I was convinced that we couldn't be anything more than friends because we'd grown up together and it wasn't going to be like the movies." She rolls her eyes. "I mean, right there is probably half of our problem. We are the movie generation."

"I thought we were millennials."

"No, we're like right on the tail end of Generation X, where we didn't grow up with social media but we're using it now to give us this picture of what our perfect little lives should look like."

I smile at Eliza. "Tell me how you really feel."

"Makes me insane. I'm about to delete everything and go back to a flip phone."

She will probably do it, too. I feel like if Eliza didn't need a phone for work, she probably wouldn't have one.

"Anyway. Just don't make having 'spark' something that it blown out of proportion. I don't know if there's any with Mike, I don't even know if he's the right person for you or not, but I know him and I know you and I think you should both give each other a chance."

"Thanks Eliza."

"And now, we are going to watch *Penelope* and pretend that Johnny Martin is coming to sing 'You Are My Sunshine' to us both."

I grin. "Deal."

I'm not working Wednesday, so I don't even set an alarm. After all these late nights, I need a day to just sleep in.

So when my eyes pop open and won't close back up at six-thirty, I get mad.

This is sad.

I am officially old. I'm about to become that old lady who gets up at five just for the sake of it and waits by the front door to chide the paper boy for being late.

I lay there until seven and finally just get up.

I remember Eliza talking about how when she can't sleep, she would always walk down the path to the park, which sounds good. I haven't gone for a run in a long time.

I think Katie is still asleep, so I quietly get dressed in my dark purple yoga capri things and a black long-sleeve jacket, brush my teeth, pull on my running shoes and sneak out the front door. The air is cool and kind of damp this morning, perfect after the hot, hot, hot humidity we've been having.

My hair instantly boings into Shirley Temple curls and I pull the hairband off my wrist and tie it up right away.

I do a couple of little stretches and start off down the path.

And like ten minutes into it, I am about to die. I slow down, heaving, putting crossing my arms over my head, trying to help my lungs expand.

Good grief, I am in terrible, terrible shape.

There's this long path through our neighborhood that leads to this little park close to the river, so I walk and scoot aside for bicycles whizzing past and smile at the people walking their hyper little dogs.

Lots of people like the early mornings, I guess.

The light is all soft and warm, the trees are shimmering with the dew. Everything feels really fresh and clean.

I'm still heaving like a broken down accordion, but I try my best to take deep breaths and slow my heart rate. Maybe I need to do some training again before I try to flat out run.

I'm so much better at regularly working out during the school year when my schedule is the exact same every single day.

I start a really slow jog.

"On your left!" A bike flies past me so I do my best to stay as far to the right of the path as I can.

The park is already full of people and dogs. A group of older ladies are slowly walking around it, a couple of younger people are running, a few others are stretching in the grass and a couple of people talk while they throw Frisbees to their dogs.

The sun is getting brighter and it's a beautiful morning.

I sit down on one of the benches and catch my breath, leaning my head back and closing my eyes for a second.

All these words are stuck in my head and I rub my temples, hearing all of them at the same time.

Let us approach the throne of grace with confidence.

Don't lay down the cross of Christ to pick up the burden of offense.

Don't toss aside the diamond in the rough for the polished and shiny rhinestone.

Apparently, people look at me these days and feel like I need a sermon. If Pastor Mark were here right now, he would probably look and me and bust right into his classic opener of, "Friend, today is a good day."

I watch some of the people throwing the Frisbees for a little bit.

The group of elderly ladies comes around the bend on the path leading around the park. There are a few younger joggers who are a few feet behind them, but closing the distance quickly. One guy in a backward baseball cap and shorts smiles warmly at the ladies as he gets close to them and I can barely hear him greeting them.

"Why hello there!" The old ladies are adorable, flirting with the guy and he slows his pace to talk to them for a bit.

"How's the shoulder, Mrs. Mabel?"

"You know, honey, I think it's going to be just fine. Thanks for asking."

"And how's the garden, Mrs. Edith?"

"Just beautiful. I'll have another bag of tomatoes for you tomorrow, Michael."

I squint from the bench and every muscle in my body kind of freezes.

Oh my gosh. It's Mike.

Mike Wakeman.

I did not even recognize him until right this second when he is basically three feet in front of me. Maybe because I've never seen him in a hat or workout clothes before, but maybe also because I've never seen that kind of a smile on him.

His whole face looks different. His eyes are all soft and gentle as he looks at the ladies, his smile warm. He even has laugh lines.

I swear, there has to be two Mikes and I've been interacting with the grumpier twin.

He grins at the gardener woman. "That sounds amazing. I finished the last bag two days ago."

"I only gave it to you three days ago!"

"They were amazing! It was like eating candy."

"Michael, darling, you should not be eating a bag of tomatoes in a day," the lady says, shaking her head. "Do you know the acidity content in tomatoes and what that can do to your stomach?"

"I'll tell you. Ulcers," another one of the ladies says.

They make the turn and start walking back up the path, away from me. I stay totally still and try to blend into the bench as best as I can.

Be the bench. You are the bench.

Mike is laughing now at something one of the ladies said and I swear, I have never heard him laugh like this. It's a warm, deep laugh and I think it fills his whole chest.

Who is this guy?

CHAPTER *Sixteen*

"Hello!"

I look up on Thursday and Eliza is standing right in front of me, grinning like someone who confused chocolate covered espresso beans for multivitamins.

I look at her, putting my order pad back in my apron pocket and half-apologize to my table as I clear their menus and move Eliza out of the way.

"Hi. I'm working."

"So, you love me, right?"

I am never comfortable when she begins conversations this way. Usually, I end up more uncomfortable later though.

"I'll say it again, Eliza. I do not want a puppy. And Katie would kill you if you do that to her again."

"No, no, no, no," Eliza says, waving her hands all emphatically, like a charismatic preacher. "No dogs are involved."

"Or a cat. We don't want a cat either."

"No members of the animal kingdom will be harmed by this venture," Eliza says. "I swear to you, this only involves you and not anything or anyone else." She kisses the three fingers on her left hand and holds them in the air.

"What is that?"

"Boy Scouts. Right?"

"Pretty sure that was *The Hunger Games* salute right before people died."

"Eh, I guess they are both applicable."

"Yeah. Whatever it is, the answer is no."

Eliza groans. "Look, I wanted to see if you wanted to meet me for coffee and dessert tonight."

"Eliza, I hate coffee and I watch you drink coffee and eat dessert basically every night. So why the special and slightly weird invitation?"

"Because, Katie is going out with Luke and I am lonely because Cooper is not only not here but he also is out of the state on a business trip, so I don't even get to talk to him and do the whole 'no, you hang up, no, you hang up' thing and I feel like we need a girls' night."

A girls' night does sound fun.

And I haven't been anywhere other than Minnie's for dessert in a long time.

I sigh. "You promise you won't talk about Mike the whole time?"

"I promise I won't say a word." She grins at me.

"Fine."

"Yay!"

"Where do you want to go?"

"Do you like tiramisu?"

I love tiramisu. "Yes."

"Know that little Italian pizza place kind of over by that tire store on Ashwood? Guido's, or something like that?"

I half-nod, but I have no idea what she's talking about. "Um. Sure."

"Right. Well, they have amazing cappuccinos and tiramisu."

"Do they have Coke?"

Eliza sighs. "Some day, Ash. Some day."

"Ah, but not today."

"Yes, they have soda too. But I guarantee the coffee tastes better."

"We can agree to disagree. What time? I get off about seven."

She shrugs. "Let's do seven, then."

"I'd kind of like to shower first. Can we do eight? Then we could ride together."

Eliza shrugs. "Eight is fine. But I'm not planning on going home between now and then."

"What are you going to do?"

"Girl, I'm getting married in like two weeks!"

"It's like four and a half months, but okay."

"I have things to do! People to see! Overpriced crap to buy!"

I laugh.

"Eight o'clock at Piero's!" She leaves.

I think Eliza might have one of those mental blocks when it comes to names. Either that, or she doesn't care.

Knowing her, I'm going to bet on the second one.

I find a tire shop on Ashwood at five minutes until eight o'clock later that night and there's a little tiny sign on the building next to it.

Lorenzo's.

I guess this is probably it.

I pull into a parking space and put on a tiny bit of the tinted chapstick I keep in my purse. Eliza wasn't dressed super fancy earlier, but she looked cute and so I didn't want to show up wearing my lounge pants like I usually put on after my post-work shower. I am actually dressed. I have on skinny jeans and a loose-knit gray shirt with my red canvas flats. I blow-dried my hair and attempted to half-style it as best I could by sort of twirling back the sides and pinning them down with bobby pins.

It's a little bit of a country-ish look for me, but at least it's sort of off my face, except for the couple of shorter pieces that are boinging around my forehead.

The last time I went to get a haircut, my stylist talked me into a "fringe", which I guess is hairdresser code for "bangs".

Needless to say, it's been six months and I have never once worn them as bangs.

Mostly because I don't have the hour it took the lady to flat-iron my hair so it actually looks decent.

I mean, during the summer, I would have to get up by three in the morning. And even if I flat-iron it, it never stays straight through the entire day, especially when the humidity is high.

Curly hair, it is.

I've seen all these blog posts and watched all these videos about how you should work with the hair God gave you and not try to change it. They are usually written and filmed by these gorgeous women who all have hair exactly like Katie's – it looks amazing no matter what they do.

Those people should not be allowed to blog.

I walk inside the restaurant and it's nice and cool in here and there's basically no one around. Eliza isn't here yet and there's a worn sign saying to "seat yourself", so I go sit at the corner booth and look around the restaurant.

Either this place is terrible or now that it's eight o'clock, we've completely missed the dinner crowd.

Hopefully it's the latter.

A kid who is probably about eighteen comes over, clearing his throat. "Hey, welcome to Lorenzo's. What can I get you to drink?"

"Coke, please."

"Sure." He leaves and returns with one of those 70's-style plastic cups that totally remind me of a super old pizzeria a few minutes later.

"Ready to order?"

"I'm waiting for my friend, actually," I say. "And I have no idea what she wants."

"Okay, cool. I'll come back when she gets here."

"Sounds great."

I feel bad for the guy. There's one other table with people at it, the rest of the restaurant is empty. I can hear people arguing in what sounds like it could be Italian in the back.

It would be an incredibly boring shift to work right now.

The bell over the door dings and Mike walks in.

Immediately, I am shaking my head and kicking myself because, good grief. I should have known.

Mike looks over, sees me shaking my head like a bobble head doll in the hands of a three year old and apparently, has the same thought I do, because he is also immediately doing the same shake.

He stands there for a second by the empty hostess stand and then walks over to my booth.

"I'm assuming you are here to meet Eliza."

I finally stop shaking my head long enough to nod to him. "You too?"

He sighs and slides into the booth.

I'm not sure who I saw at the park yesterday morning, but it was not this Mike.

This Mike is the same Mike I know. Frown lines and all.

He rubs a hand through his hair and looks at me, sighing again. "Well. I guess this explains why she didn't want me to pick her up."

"You offered too?"

He kind of does this like half-laugh, half-huff. "Well. Have you eaten?"

I had half a sandwich at Minnie's and a cookie.

But that was around four o'clock. And I'm not sure if it counted for lunch or dinner.

"Not really," I say.

"Me either and I'm starving." He looks at me and it's almost shyness in his expression. "Would you like to…maybe have dinner?" he asks.

Here's the thing. I've always thought Mike was a decent looking person. Not necessarily cute, but nice enough looking.

That expression, though, is adorable.

His eyes are all soft and he's nervously rubbing his five o'clock shadow with one hand.

And all of a sudden, there are all these tiny little beads jumping around in my stomach, like I swallowed a can of elementary school art supplies.

I can feel my cheeks warming and I look down at the table, clearing my throat. "Uh, sure, that, I mean, that sounds great. I mean, we're...uh, already here, so we um...we might as well. Right?"

"Right." Mike smiles at me and I think it might be the first smile I've ever seen on him when he's looking at me that doesn't involve any sort of sarcasm or eye rolling or would probably be considered a half-frown.

I don't know what happened to Mike, but I'm almost more wanting to leave now than I was when I was anticipating frowning Mike. At least with him, I knew exactly where I stood. The soft smiling, shy Mike is really making me feel off-kilter over here.

"Hi." Waiter kid is back and I use the break to inhale as quietly as I can, though I really want to pull a Westley and Buttercup escaping from the "lightning sand" moment right there.

"What can I get you to drink?"

"I'll have Coke too, please."

"Sure. Ready to order?"

I haven't even seen a menu, so I have no idea what they have.

"I'm not sure we've seen a menu yet," Mike says.

"Ah. First timers," the kid says. "They're behind the salt and pepper. I'll be back with your Coke."

He leaves and Mike pulls two menus from where they were hiding between the salt and pepper and a little tray filled with assorted jellies.

I see these trays all the time at different restaurants. Grandma Minnie thinks they are a travesty and never fails to tell people that. "You don't know when the last time they changed them, you don't know how many slobbery nine month olds have used them as teethers and then stuck them back. Nope. We will not do that."

Instead, Grandma Minnie has a list in the menu of the homemade jams and jellies she offers.

I open the tiny menu and apparently, Lorenzo's believes in offering only a few things. Which is fine.

My stomach isn't really feeling up to par anyway, now. Maybe it's better if I eat a light dinner.

"What are you thinking?" Mike asks.

Honestly, I'm thinking that it's weird how different Mike can be but I don't really want to say that out loud.

So I sort of hum a little, "Mm, I don't know" and hope he leaves it alone.

"Not an Italian food fan?"

"Oh, you meant what am I thinking I'll order?"

"Um. Yeah."

"Oh. Probably the fettuccine alfredo."

"I thought that sounded good too. What did you think I meant? Just what you are thinking in general?"

Maybe it's better to be completely honest. It's not like we are dating, or really even friends, so I don't think there's any harm in telling him.

Besides, if God says I can approach Him, the creator of everything, with confidence, then surely I can talk to Mike.

All he's created is some turmoil.

I set my menu down with purpose and Mike looks at me. "So, you're different tonight, uh, than you sometimes are," I state and he looks at me.

"Like, I look different?" He rubs his chin again. "I need to shave."

"No, no, it's not that. You aren't, um..."

"Tired?"

"Frowning."

He nods, slowly. "Eliza is always telling me I frown a lot, too. I don't feel like I do, but maybe I do more than I think."

"Why do you?"

262

"Why do I what?"

"Frown?"

He leans back, giving a little half-laugh again. "You don't beat around the bush, do you?"

Waiter kid is back, we give him our orders, he nods and leaves.

"I'm sorry," I tell him as soon as the guy is out of ear shot. "I shouldn't have said anything."

Goodness knows, I don't want to scare off this non-frowning Mike and have the frowning one return.

He lets his breath out and shakes his head. "No, it's fine."

"We don't have to talk about it," I say, quickly, waving my hands. "I...this is nice. I mean, I like that you aren't frowning. I mean...oh my goodness."

He grins at my obvious distress. I think the heat radiating off my face is singeing the few hairs that have fallen out of the bobby pins.

"You're funny, Ashten."

I sigh. "Thanks."

"Look, I think we might have gotten off on the wrong foot," Mike says, slowly.

I nod. "Possibly."

He looks at me for a long minute and then reaches across the table, hand open. "Hi. I'm Mike Wakeman."

I laugh and he smiles, but he keeps his hand there, half nodding to it.

I set my hand in his, shaking it lightly. "Ashten Wadeley."

His hands are pretty rough but warm. He shakes my hand for slightly longer than necessary and there is no trace of the person who said "despite everything" in his smile. "Nice to meet you, Ashten."

He gently lets go of my hand and I immediately clasp my hands together under the table.

Mike is smiling and sweet and they set these giant plates of pasta covered in cream sauce and freshly grated Parmesan in front of us and I realize it.

I am on a date.

With Mike Wakeman.

"What's wrong?" Mike asks me after the waiter kid leaves.

I shake my head. "Nothing."

"Can I pray?" He holds a hand out again and I bite my bottom lip before reaching over.

This is twice in like five minutes that I have held Mike's hand.

So not only am I on a date with Mike, I am now holding his hand.

Again.

I am very grateful that you are supposed to close your eyes and duck your head to pray. At least then, I can pretend that I'm not purposefully avoiding eye contact.

This is too weird.

I mean, I don't even know what is going on here. Is Mike bipolar? Is he a twin and I keep running into the grumpy one, like that magician movie that I can't remember the name of? Is this some horrible April's Fools joke and I'm going to start to like the new Mike only to discover that the real Mike is the old Mike?

Or maybe Eliza is right and Mike is actually like this one – nice, sweet. Possibly even funny.

I don't hear one word of Mike's prayer.

"Amen," he says and I yank my hand away like he has leprosy or something.

A brief frown skitters across his face but he's quick to neutralize it, picking up his fork. "I've never been here before, but this looks great," he says.

"Um, yeah. Me too."

"Hey, so do you feel like you've gotten to know Cooper pretty well now?"

Seriously, I feel like I'm in some sort of twilight zone.

"Um, sure, sure," I say.

"Oh good. He's a great guy. Don't tell him I said that. But he's basically my brother. I've been waiting and praying for him and Eliza to get together for about ten years."

On and on he talks about Eliza, about Cooper, about the way they grew up, about how they were all super close, especially after Cooper's mom left.

Somehow he even finishes his entire plate of fettuccine and bread the waiter kid dropped off too.

Meanwhile, I'm barely making it through half my pasta, which is sad, because everyone knows that fettuccine alfredo does not make good leftovers.

The waiter kid is back and takes Mike's empty plate. "Can I bring you dessert?" he asks. "We only make one dessert and it's our tiramisu. Perhaps one to share?"

Mike looks at me and I am torn.

On the one hand, that's the main reason I came here tonight.

On the other hand, my appetite is totally gone.

I don't know why. Maybe it's sitting here with Mike 2.0.

Here's the thing. If I had met this Mike first, I would have said yes to a date with him in a heartbeat. He's sweet, he's funny, he hasn't seemed the least bit annoyed or ticked off and he hasn't snorted once even though the waiter has implied many times that we are on a date.

"Sure," Mike says, shrugging to the kid. "Tiramisu sounds great. Could I get a decaf coffee with that, too?"

"Sure thing. Ma'am?"

"No thanks."

"Oh yeah, I think Eliza mentioned that you hate coffee," Mike says, after the waiter leaves again.

"I don't hate it, I just don't like it very much. I don't like any hot drinks."

"Have you tried iced coffee?"

"I'd really much rather drink a Coke."

"Good to know. I won't ask you to go to Starbucks with me."

I am immediately thinking of when he basically snooped on my entire date with Daniel at Starbucks and I guess he is too, because he frowns slightly, opens his mouth like he's going to say something and then lightly shakes his head.

"You can ask," I say.

"Does that guy know you hate coffee?"

"I don't hate it, I just—"

Mike grins and interrupts. "Dislike it. Right. Does he know you don't like it?"

Daniel isn't really one for noticing things. Case in point, church. It probably never crossed his mind that I might not want him at my new church and especially sitting right next to me.

"I don't know, actually," I say.

Mike fiddles with a straw wrapper and I know he wants to ask more about him.

"Go ahead and ask," I say. Again.

Mike smiles at my constant prompting. "Sorry, just trying to gauge the situation here. So, you guys are or are not dating?"

"We are not." I don't think I can say this fast enough.

The immediately relief on Mike's face is really cute.

No, no, Ashten! Do not go there!

I stuff down my inner voice with some fettuccine.

"Okay, cool," Mike says. "So, he's some random guy?"

"We used to date."

"I see."

"Like a year ago."

"Okay."

"And then he moved to Alaska."

"For the sled dogs?"

"For a job. But I guess he's back."

"And you guys are not dating?"

"No."

Mike looks at me, obviously remembering the awful church service too. "Does he know that?"

I sigh. "I'm pretty sure." I was a hundred percent sure until Sunday.

A slice of tiramisu bigger than my head is set on the table in front of us and we both balk at it.

"Enjoy." The waiter leaves and Mike shakes his head.

"I'm glad we didn't get two."

I smile.

268

The evening passes so fast and before I know it, it's ten o'clock and the place is basically kicking us out. Mike pays for dinner, despite my protests to pay for my own and he holds the door open for me as we leave.

Everything is covered in this silvery glow from the full moon outside and I smile up at it, thinking about Eliza and her superstitions about full moons and babies being born. She's always a huge grouch when it's a full moon and she has to work. "Anyone working labor and delivery or on the mother baby floor should be getting paid overtime for full moon nights," she always grouses.

"Hey, so, I know this wasn't exactly either of our plan for tonight, but I had a good time," Mike says and he's not even snorting or insulting me or anything.

I want to ask him. I want to ask him so badly about the "despite everything" line, but I also don't want to kill the mood. Or end what has turned into a really nice evening on a bad note. And I'm working tomorrow and I'm officially like an hour past when I try to get in bed on work nights.

So, opening up a long discussion is probably not my best move for tomorrow.

I keep my mouth shut.

Mike shoves his hands in his pockets like he doesn't really know what to do with them and I actually kind of like that's he's feeling awkward here too.

"Thank you for dinner," I say.

"Thanks for coming." Then he kind of laughs. "Or, I guess, thanks for not leaving right away when I got here."

I smile.

Then we both stand there all weirdly and the awkwardness is seriously making my toes hurt.

"Well," I say.

"Anyway," he says, right at the same time.

We both kind of laugh that little chuckle that you do when something like that happens and I kind of want to pull out my phone and Google whether or not you can die from awkwardness.

Because I seriously might.

"Have a good night, Ashten," Mike says. He pulls a hand out of his pocket and steps toward me like he might be going to either squeeze my hand or give me a hug or something, but then he stops halfway there.

So now, we're standing way too close together for no reason at all.

I seriously feel like I just swallowed a bag of glitter.

My throat is all choky and scratchy, my stomach feels like I'm going to be seasick and I can't get a full breath.

Mike looks down at me and his eyelashes scrunch together a touch and his eyes soften and I know, I just *know*, he's going to kiss me.

"Well, see you later!" I sound like a cheerleader chipmunk and I run for my car and jump inside.

270

I can't even breathe in here.

I roll down the windows right away and grip the steering wheel with both hands, inhaling through my nose and exhaling through my clenched teeth.

I don't even know what just happened.

I drive home and I still can't swallow. I park in my driveway, walk up the front walk, unlock the door, close it behind me and sit down on the couch.

Katie and Eliza are sitting at what used to be our kitchen table, but it appears that it was eaten by some sort of Abominable Tulle Monster. They both look at me, look at each other and are immediately up and next to me on the couch.

"How did it go?" Eliza asks.

"Are you okay?" Katie asks. Based on the way she says it, I know she has been updated as to my evening's activities.

"What do you need?"

"Are you okay?"

"Did he pay for you?"

"Are you okay?"

"Did you have fun? Did he talk? Was he nice?"

Katie holds my hand. "Are you okay?" I think she's stuck on repeat.

I wave them both off, stand up and go in the kitchen for some water to flush down the last of the glitter that is stuck in my throat.

They both follow me like I'm the Mother Duck.

"Ash?"

"You okay, honey?"

I take a long swig of the water and turn to the two of them who are both standing there all big-eyed like two of the Precious Moments dolls my Grandma Minnie has collected over the years.

"I'm okay," I tell Katie.

She exhales. "Good."

"How was Mike?" Eliza asks.

"He was...nice."

Eliza grins. "I was hoping he was going to behave."

"No, I mean, he was really nice. Polite. He was even funny at certain times."

I think if Eliza owned fireworks, she would be shooting them off right now, but she settles for this weird little interpretive dance instead.

I watch her for a minute and now I can maybe see a little bit of why Mike seems to have two personalities.

I mean, he did grow up with this.

I would probably be grouchy half the time, too. Eliza is like this from the second her eyes open in the morning until she goes to sleep.

If someone woke me up like this, I would probably be in the papers the next morning.

"So, what are you going to do?" Katie asks me.

"What do you mean?"

"I mean, are you going to go out again with him?"

We never discussed it, so I don't know. I sort of shrug. "He didn't ask."

"He didn't ask?!" Eliza is aghast. "Good grief. Sorry, Ash. He's so dumb sometimes. He doesn't have a lot of practice dating."

"That's not really a bad thing," I say. I can already see the wheels turning in Eliza's head and I am shaking my head. "Don't do anything, Eliza. Just let it play out. Please."

"Listen to the woman," Katie commands. "You've meddled enough."

"Hey, but it worked!" The interpretive dance is back and Eliza shimmies around the kitchen, grinning. "Dude, I am the best!"

I look at her, look at Katie and take another long drink of my water. "I'm going to bed."

"Wait! Aren't you going to dish? We haven't even hardly talked about this!" Eliza protests.

"I have to be up and out the door in six hours," I tell her. "Unlike you, with your vampire genes, I have to sleep."

She grins. "Hey, did you see the moon tonight?"

"Yep."

"Did you also see who is *not* working?"

She seriously looks like a bad try out for *Hairspray*.

"Good night, Eliza."

"Night, Ash!"

Katie smiles at me, shaking her head at Eliza. "Night, Ash. Sweet dreams."

I brush my teeth, wash my face and go to my room. I change into my pajamas and climb under the covers, pulling over my Bible.

By this point, my Bible automatically opens to Hebrews.

Therefore let us draw near with confidence to the throne of grace, so that we may receive mercy and find grace to help in time of need.

I turn off the light and pull the covers up around my neck.

I realize that one blind date isn't really that big of a deal, but for some reason, it feels like a big deal. Maybe because it's Mike. Maybe because we know each other outside of this blind date and his sister is one of my best friends. If nothing comes of this, it's going to be awkward for the rest of our lives.

But on the flip side, if something does come of this, it's going to be awkward for the rest of our lives, because why was I an acceptable date tonight but not a few weeks ago? And why the whole "despite everything" line?

274

Jesus, if You're still offering, I could really use some of that grace to help. I would classify this as a time of need.

CHAPTER *Seventeen*

"Ashten? Can I speak with you?"

Part of me knew this moment was coming.

I look over at Grandma Minnie and she has both flour-covered hands on her hips.

This is never a good sign.

"Yes, ma'am."

I set the coffee pot back on the warmer and walk over, feeling a little like a lost dog with it's tail between it's legs.

She nods to the stool next to her work station, where she has been cutting out rolls for about an hour already.

"Sit."

Now I feel even more like a dog, but I listen and obey. "Yes, ma'am." I sit on the stool and look at her.

"You have been slamming around here all morning," Grandma Minnie starts. "Now, I am in complete understanding about not being a morning person. It took me twenty-five years before I wasn't breaking the snooze button on my alarm clock. But, darling, you need to figure out how to put a smile on that face and stop snapping at your cousins."

"Yes, ma'am."

"And when a customer asks for more biscuits, you give them more biscuits without any sort of eye rolling."

"Yes, ma'am."

Grandma Minnie sighs and then sits down on the barstool next to me, reaching for my wrist. "What is going on, Ashten?"

I look at my grandmother and for some reason, tears start building in my eyes.

"I had a date last night," I tell her, trying to be extra quiet because goodness only knows that my father does not need to find this out right now.

She looks at me and rubs my shoulder. "I'm sorry. It didn't go well?"

"No, it went good."

Tears are dropping out of my eyes and landing on my cheeks and I kind of half-laugh, swiping my face with the back of my hand while I am sniffing away.

Grandma Minnie makes a face at me and then hands me the dishtowel that was on the counter next to her rolled out dough.

I start mopping up my face and nose. "Thanks."

"You know, honey, it's been a long, long time since I went on a date, but I don't remember crying after the good ones."

"It was with Mike."

"Mike is one of those boys who keeps coming in here."

"He's the one who said 'despite everything'."

Grandma Minnie smiles. "Ah-ha."

"Yeah."

"I'm actually impressed that you went on a date with him."

"Well, it was a blind date and I didn't know I was meeting him, so it wasn't exactly by choice."

"But it went well."

"Yes."

"I assume he didn't say anything like he's said before then."

I shake my head. "No, he was really kind and sweet. He actually even smiled."

"Smiling is good," Grandma Minnie says. "It's something you should do a little more of today."

"I just don't get it," I say. "He's normally so closed off. I don't understand why he was so different last night."

Grandma Minnie shrugs. "I don't know. Why are you so grouchy today? People have the ability to change. Sometimes for the good, sometimes for the bad. Maybe you've never caught him at a good time."

"He didn't even insult me at all."

Grandma Minnie looks at me. "Well, did you ask him about the day he told you he liked you?"

"No."

"Ashten, did you ever think about the throne of grace, like we talked about?"

I blink at the abrupt change in the conversation. "Um, yeah, I have been thinking of it a lot."

"Well, what was the conclusion you came to?"

"The conclusion about what?"

Grandma Minnie reaches for her dough cutter. She isn't really the type to sit still, even if she's having a conversation. "Let us approach the throne of grace with confidence," she paraphrases. "What did you decide that meant?"

"Doesn't it mean that we can always come to God?"

She nods. "Yes. But in order to understand it, we need to look at the verses ahead of it. Jesus came to earth and was tempted in everything. He experienced everything we have and will ever know. He knew what it feels like to be insulted or looked down upon. Goodness, during his first miracles, people were constantly saying things like, 'Isn't this that woodworker kid? He's just nothing!'"

I nod and Grandma Minnie smiles at me.

"Honey, what I'm trying to say is that our confidence isn't found in confidence alone or even in knowing our position as a child of God. Our confidence is found in knowing that our God knows not only us, but He has experienced life on earth and He is willing and able and wants to give us grace and help when we need it."

She stands up and pats my shoulder. "And sweetheart, you need some grace and help today."

"I'm sorry, Grandma."

She smiles at me. "I love you, Ashten honey. Now go take your orders out before your brother has a fit."

"Yes, ma'am."

I go load up a tray and take them out to my table, trying my best to seem happier and cheerful.

Inside, though, I'm praying constantly.

Lord, I need grace. I need help.

And if possible, I really need this confusion to end.

I don't know why I'm so rattled.

Maybe because, for the first time possibly ever, I liked Mike.

Like actually *liked* him.

Which brings up a whole bunch of other issues, because the last guy I liked, up and moved to Alaska.

Maybe there is something about me that sends people running. Maybe that's the *despite everything* that Mike was talking about.

Maybe, the full sentence was supposed to be, "Despite the fact that you repel people, I still like you."

Grace please, Jesus!

By two o'clock, I am done and I think Will knows it. My head is pounding so hard my eyes are starting to get those little black dots in my peripherals.

I close out a check and Will is in front of me by the computer. "Go home."

"I'm scheduled until six."

"I'm sending you home early. This is ridiculous. You look like death. People are going to think they are going to catch some sort of plague from you."

I rub my head and I'm too tired to argue. "Okay."

"Good. Go sleep or something. I don't know what's going on, but you need to chill or something, Ash."

Meet my brother, the King of Sympathy.

I drive home and Katie is sitting at the kitchen table, laptop open in front of her and a bowl of leftover taco meat with melted cheese on top next to it.

She looks at the clock and then at me. "You're home early! Slow day? Wow, are you okay?"

"Apparently, I look like death so I got sent home early."

"You do kind of look like death. Are you feeling okay? I have some sort of immune support vitamins around here somewhere." She jumps up and starts going through the kitchen cabinets.

I shake my head. "I'm fine. I need to think. Or not think. Or something. I don't know."

Katie pauses by the open cabinet and just looks at me. "Hey Ash? Have you ever walked along that path by the river?"

I nod. "Once or twice."

"You should go back. Just walk and think and pray. Bring your Bible. I think what you really need is to spend some time with Jesus."

She's right. I know she's right.

I go change out of my work clothes and pull on a pair of yoga capris and a tunic-length gray shirt. My hair is already up and I grab my Bible and my sneakers.

"See you in awhile," Katie says, handing me a paper sack as I come back through the kitchen.

"Thanks."

I get in the car and set the bag next to me on the seat, driving the ten or so minutes to the river. There's a little parking lot along the busiest part of the downtown area and I park the car there, go through the flood wall and start walking up the path, Bible and paper sack in hand.

I haven't looked in the sack yet, but knowing Katie, she's not going to want me to open it until I'm also opening my Bible.

I'm amazed at how crowded it is here, especially considering it's three o'clock on a Friday afternoon. Bikes are everywhere, families are out, skipping rocks into the Mississippi. The few benches I pass are occupied, old couples talking about the good old days, young moms trying to feed wild little toddlers a snack, young couples holding hands and watching the river.

Part of me is like, good for you all! Taking a break, getting outside, embracing the life of the French! And part of me is like, what in the world do all of you do for a living that you can be out here at three o'clock on a workday?

Though, I guess I'm here and I work a lot.

I keep walking and the crowds thin more and more the farther from the parking area I get. I'm assuming I'm about a mile or two up the river and I finally find an empty bench under a few trees, a little ways off the path but where I can still see the river. A giant barge is being moved down the Mississippi, which isn't really a rare sight, but I know at least my father has always found it fascinating.

"Just imagine how tough that little tugboat has to be!" he would always tell us, growing up.

I sit down on the bench and look at the water.

Jesus, why am I so freaked out about everything right now?

I'm not normally like this. Going on a decent date with someone doesn't usually turn me into an emotional basket case.

Maybe it's because I thought I couldn't stand Mike and he turned out to be okay?

Or maybe it's because Daniel is suddenly back too and it's throwing me completely off?

Or maybe it's because I've been up late almost constantly between the wedding planning and everything going on in the evenings and then getting up at 4am and now, I'm so sleep deprived I can't even think straight.

The barge slowly moves down the river and everything is so peaceful here that it seems weird to have been so stressed out even moments ago.

I look over at the bag on the bench next to me and pull it into my lap, unfolding the top of it.

Inside, Katie had packed an apple, a dark chocolate bar, a small composition notebook and a pen. I open the cover and her writing fills the first line on the first page and I realize it is a writing prompt.

Where do I find my identity?

I read her careful, neat handwriting and instant tears blur in my eyes.

I look up at the river, blinking.

I know what I would like to write down. I would love to write the good, Christian response.

My identity is in Christ.

I watch the barge.

Ah, but it's not, is it, Lord?

Everything is quiet, everything is calm. And I know, somehow, that I am not alone here on this bench.

284

I think about even the last several weeks.

So much has happened in such a short amount of time.

I don't even know where it all began. Maybe on my birthday. Maybe it's this nagging feeling I have that I should have more or have accomplished more or even *be* more by now.

I'm thirty-one years old and I have nothing to show for it.

I can feel the prick in my soul and the tears keep on coming.

Is that really true?

When I was younger, I knew exactly what I thought I would have or have done by now. I'd have a house. A husband. Probably a couple of kids. I'd probably have taken a leave of absence from the teaching to stay home with my own children while they were babies, possibly raise them in the restaurant like I was raised.

And instead...

Instead I have me. I am close to having the house, but not quite. I am not close to having a husband and I am what feels like light years away from having the kids.

Jesus, is that it?

Maybe, the issue isn't Daniel or Mike or the "despite everything". Maybe the issue is that deep down, I already felt I'm lacking in who I am.

Just me.

Maybe, the issue isn't even marriage or kids, though they both sound nice.

Let us approach the throne of grace with confidence.

What if the confidence isn't my own pride? What if the confidence isn't my feelings about Christ that day or how successful I am at picking myself up and reminding myself of the confidence I need to have? What if the confidence the Bible is talking about has nothing to do with *confidence* like I interpret the word, but has absolutely nothing to do with me at all?

I look at Katie's question again.

Identity.

Maybe I can approach God's throne with confidence, not because of who I am or what I've done or how Christian I am or how often I read the Bible or pray or go to church or listen to Christian radio or whatever...

Maybe I can approach the throne with confidence because of who *He* is.

And it has nothing to do with me.

Maybe *my* identity needs to not be mine at all.

I sit and watch the river for a long, long time.

CHAPTER *Eighteen*

The house is empty when I get home. Which doesn't bother me at all.

My head kind of hurts from all this thinking.

I get in the shower and let the hot water hit the back of my neck and close my eyes.

I feel different somehow.

And I'm not sure how. I don't know if I can even define how or why I feel this way, but I do.

I feel peace deep in my heart, deep in my lungs for the first time in I can't even remember how long. I feel like I can breathe easily. Finally.

I blow dry my hair, skip the makeup and pull on my softest lounge pants and a purple sweatshirt.

I am going to sit and watch a movie.

Going through my DVDs, I find *Sabrina*, something I haven't watched in years and years. I think the last time I watched it was with Grandma Minnie.

I look at the clock, it's almost seven.

Surely she's home.

Grandpa John answers the phone. "Hello?"

"Hey Grandpa. It's Ashten."

"Ashten! How's my favorite granddaughter?"

I grin. Grandpa John says this to all of his granddaughters.

"I'm doing good. Hey, is Grandma there?"

"Yep, yep, she is. Hang on a second, honey."

A minute later, my grandmother gets on the phone. "Hello?"

"Hey Grandma."

"Ashten! How are you, sweetheart?"

"Good. Hey, are you doing anything tonight?"

"No, no, I think we are going to be at home. Why? Did you need something?"

"Would you like to watch a movie with me? I was thinking about watching *Sabrina*."

"With Harrison Ford?"

"That's the one."

"Well, darling, I have had a rule for about, oh, forty-something years and it's treated me well for all of them."

"What's that, Grandma?"

"Never turn down watching a movie when Harrison Ford is in it."

I laugh.

"The man is dreamy."

I can hear my grandfather in the background. "Well, thank you, Min."

"Not you, dear."

Poor Grandpa John.

"So yes, that sounds lovely. Would you like me to come there?"

I know that Grandma Minnie drives almost every day in the dark to the restaurant, but my dad and several of my uncles have told me that it terrifies them to think of Grandpa John and Grandma Minnie driving when it isn't light out.

"No, I can come there!" I say. It's not dark yet, but it will be soon.

"Okay, honey. We'll see you in a few minutes."

"Bye."

I hang up, find my UGG boots and my purse. It might be summer time, but I am going to dress cozy.

I run through the grocery store on my way over and Grandpa John meets me at the door. "Well, what in the world did you bring, Ashten? Minnie only said you were bringing a movie."

"I got some snacks for us."

I unload the bags onto their kitchen counter. Ice cream, popcorn, Milky Ways. I almost grabbed Oreos, but Grandma Minnie thinks packaged cookies are of the devil.

Grandma Minnie walks into the kitchen then, fluffing her hair.

"Goodness, Ashten, what on earth?"

"Well, I figured we should have some snacks."

"Me too, that's why I pulled out the cookies."

I look over and Grandma Minnie has a bag of pre-portioned frozen chocolate chip cookie dough out on the counter.

I grin.

"Oven is preheating, they should be ready in just a bit. Shall we start it?"

I know my grandparents are going to be up early for the Saturday shift tomorrow. The weekends are anything but restful for them.

I think I'm scheduled through lunch tomorrow. Then I have Sunday off.

Grandpa John puts the DVD in the player, Grandma Minnie puts the cookies in the oven and I snuggle down on their couch with a blanket. Grandpa John sits on my right and then Grandma Minnie comes in and sits on my left.

I grin.

"What?" Grandma Minnie says, seeing my smile.

"Nothing. This is fun."

She looks at me for a long minute and her eyes warm. "You finally figured it out," she declares.

I smile.

The movie comes on and Grandma Minnie pats my knee. I know that means we will talk later.

This time, I'm actually excited to.

Sabrina comes on the screen and she's adorable, way too adorable for the mess that is David and then Harrison Ford sweeps in and steals the rest of the movie.

Grandma Minnie is sighing through half of his scenes and Grandpa John keeps rolling his eyes.

"I swear, Ashten," he says when the movie ends.

I look over at him, stuffed to the gills with cookies and ice cream. I didn't even bother with the popcorn.

"Your grandmother and I have been married for sixty-one years. We have raised four boys, built a thriving business from the ground up and to be honest, I've completely lost count of how many grandchildren and grandchildren-in-law we have now. She's my best friend and the love of my life and I've told her that every day since she was fourteen. But Ashten, mark my words, if Harrison Ford walked through the door right now and proposed to her, she'd leave me in less than a second."

"Oh come now," Grandma Minnie says, swatting the air and standing. "It would take me at least five minutes to pack the things I would want to bring with me. I could at least talk to you for those five minutes."

I leave laughing.

"See you in the morning, sweetheart," Grandpa John says, walking me to my car and then waving as I drive off.

I love my grandparents.

Saturday is almost the tiniest bit cool when I leave for work.

The promise of fall is in the air, which means my summer at Minnie's is coming to yet another end.

Part of me is sad.

Most of me is happy to get to sleep until six-thirty every day again. Plus, there's something exciting and fun about a new class with new students and new things to learn.

It's time.

Minnie's is packed today, probably due to the slight change in the weather. Anytime we have any sort of climate change, everyone freaks out and comes to the diner to eat. It's like people stop being able to feed themselves.

"Ash! Order up!"

I load up my tray for the seven-top table I have in the back of the restaurant and toss the coffee pot on there so I can start refilling the rest of my section's cups. People are going through coffee like it's water in the Sahara today.

"Good Lord, was there a news story that broke about a coffee shortage coming up or something?" Grandma Minnie grouses as I come back into the back with a dry pot.

I start another batch brewing and grin at her. "I don't know. You're the ones who watch the news."

"Someone showed up at my house with my Hollywood crush, so I had to watch that instead."

I laugh.

"Ash!"

I carry out the next table's orders and Michelle is seating him in my section.

He pops up when he sees me walk out.

"Hi Ashten."

"Hello Daniel."

It looks like he might have even gotten a haircut. He at least trimmed up the beard. And he's wearing a suit jacket over his jeans.

It's Saturday. No one wears that on Saturday.

"What can I get you?" I ask him, pulling out the notebook.

I don't know what it is. Maybe it's knowing more of where I stand with Jesus, but I look at Daniel and I don't feel anything.

All the confusion, the sadness, the loss. It's gone.

Thanks Lord.

"Is now a bad time to talk?"

293

I look around because every table in this entire building is full of hungry people dying of thirst and part of me wants to be like, "Um, *duh*," but I refrain.

"It's not a good time to talk," I tell him. "But I can bring you something to eat."

"Well, I actually came here to talk."

Maybe the altitude change from Alaska to here has caused some sort of hearing or cognitive issues for Daniel. Because it seems like regardless of what I say, it doesn't seem to matter.

Not the best impression to leave on a girl, especially if you are trying to win her back, like Daniel appears to be doing.

"We will have to do that later," I say again. "Now. Coffee?"

"Look, Ash, I was so stupid."

And apparently, we are doing this. I can hear Will yelling another order up in the back and I'm willing to bet it's mine and now he's going to be mad.

I look at Daniel and part of me feels bad for him. He's got this little lost puppy look in his eyes and I know that he genuinely feels like he made a mistake.

But God didn't.

"Daniel," I say, because if he needs it said directly in the middle of this restaurant, then he's going to get it said directly in the middle of this restaurant. "I'm sorry. I know

294

you would like to pick back up, but we can't. It's over. I've moved on and you should too."

He looks crushed. "To that other guy?"

"No. I've just moved on."

"To who?"

"Daniel. You don't always have to move on to a different person."

"So you're just going to be single?"

I shrug. "I guess that's not up to me. But please. For your own dignity, stop. Go back to Alaska. Or stay here. I don't care. But please, stop doing this."

He blinks and I realize that in our entire relationship, I have never once spoken to him like this. Even when he broke it off. I kind of stammered an, "okay, if that's what you want" and that's how we left it.

He nods to me. "You've changed."

"I hope so."

He sighs and smiles slightly at me. "Bye, Ashten."

"Bye, Daniel."

He leaves, I go in the back and Will gives me the stink eye.

"Sorry, sorry," I say. "I'm going, I'm going." I back away with my tray like it's a peace offering that was rejected.

I get back out to the tables, unload the tray and
Michelle is seating someone else in Daniel's abandoned
table.

And it's Mike.

I have to laugh.

"What?" he asks, when I come over, still smirking.

"Nothing. Just little inside joke."

"An inside joke with who? Yourself?" He gets this little
half-smile. "I guess that technically would be an *inside* inside
joke then, right?"

I roll my eyes. "Funny."

"Thanks."

"What do you want to drink?"

"Coffee, please."

There's no trace of the frown today. I smile at him as I
leave to go get the coffee pot.

There's like this weird thing in the air in this place
right now.

Grandma Minnie looks up at me as I pull the coffee pot
back out.

"Great song," she says.

"What are you talking about?"

"The one you're humming?"

"Oh." I hadn't actually realized I was.

Good grief.

I am becoming my own cliché.

She looks at me and this huge smile comes over her face. "Wait a second."

"Grandma—"

"Does this mean that—"

"Grandma—"

"He's here, isn't he?"

I sigh. "Yes," I say, after a minute, as quietly as possible, because God forbid my father walk in and hear this conversation. "Mike is here."

"I knew it, I knew it!" She points at me with her flour-covered hand. "Well, go give him coffee!"

"Yes, ma'am."

I leave and I can hear her laughing as I walk out.

Eliza is sitting at the table with Mike when I come back out and she grins at me. "Hello, friend."

"Hey!" I don't even ask, I pour her a cup too.

I set the coffee pot down on the table and try to still my hands. I'm suddenly super nervous and I have no idea why.

It's weird. It's like there's this whole strange thing that happened a few nights ago and now, I have no idea how to act around him.

But goodness, he looks cute today. He's wearing faded jeans and this long-sleeve T-shirt with the sleeves pushed up and his hair looks like he got out of the shower, dried it with the towel and then forgot to comb it.

I like it.

And it totally looks like it's Saturday and he's relaxing.

His brown eyes go all crinkly on the corners and I realize I am supposed to be writing down Eliza's order that she is rattling off and I have no idea what she just said.

I blink and look at her. "Sorry, what?"

"Dude. I listed like twelve different things. I really have to repeat it?"

"Well, I didn't know you were starting already."

"You had your pen all ready to go, I figured you were ready!"

"What do you want, Eliza?"

Mike grins.

I will not look, I will not look.

But really. The guy should have been smiling like this years ago. He has one of the nicest smiles I've ever seen.

Eliza sighs and rolls her eyes. "I want the French toast with the strawberries. *But*, I do not want powdered sugar. I'd like whipped cream and I want bacon on the side. Oh! And the fresh fruit. Oh! And those cheesy hashbrown things that Mike got that one time."

I write it down, only half hearing it, so hopefully I'm getting it right. It is really hard to concentrate right now and Mike has to be dying in that long-sleeve shirt because it's like one hundred and sixteen degrees in here.

"And um, for you?" I ask, looking up and trying not to make eye contact.

His brown eyes are twinkling.

Well, that lasted all of about .03 seconds.

He smiles at me. "I'll do the two eggs scrambled with the whole grain toast."

"Anything, uh, on the...toast?"

"What kind of jams does Minnie have today?"

I swear that he is enjoying this. He's all leaning forward, hands clasped around the coffee cup, looking for all the world like the picture of ease.

And here I am. Melting into a puddle from the heat in my cheeks and I think I have new sympathy for those poor people stricken by God at the Tower of Babel, because nothing resembling English is in my brain anymore.

I stare at him because I know he asked what kind of jams Minnie has, but for the life of me, all I can think of is telling him that she usually listens to Frank Sinatra, but sometimes she likes the new contemporary country or Christian radio.

And I feel like it's a weird question for him to be asking in relation to toast.

"Earth to Ashten!" Eliza yells.

Mike's lips are mashed shut, a smile is totally flirting all around them and his eyes are sparkling like crazy.

Has he always looked like this? Surely he hasn't.
Maybe he just got back from one of those game show things
where they do a makeover.

Or, you know, it could be the absence of the frown.

"I'll go find out," I say and leave because I have no idea
what else to do.

I walk into the back and Grandma Minnie is standing
there, grinning at me.

"So," she says.

"Jams, jams. He wants to know about jams."

She looks at me. "Well, honey...Did you tell him there's
a list in the menu?"

"Of jams?" My brain can't get off the music track. I
mean, it has been awhile since I've actually read the menu,
but I do not remember music in it.

"Sweetheart, yes. Remember? Strawberry, blackberry,
apricot?"

"Oh, *jams*!" I say, drawing the word out. It finally
clicks.

Of course, there's a list in the menu. There has always
been a list in the menu. I'm shaking my head and I walk back
out there. I can hear Grandma Minnie laughing behind me,
which, honestly, doesn't help.

"Hello," I say, walking up to their table again.

Eliza is looking at me like I have lost my mind.

Maybe I have.

"Are you okay?" she asks me.

"I'm good. So there's a list in the menu," I tell Mike. "Of the jams."

"Which one would you recommend?" he asks me, because apparently being difficult is his mission today.

I cannot remember what any of them taste like but I don't think any of them are bad.

"They're all good," I say.

I feel like he is enjoying this.

"Let's go with apricot," he says. "And can I add a side of the fruit?"

"Sure. On the side?"

He grins.

"Seriously, what is going on with you?" Eliza is shaking her head.

"I'll be back with more coffee and your food in a little bit."

I think I break Olympic records sprinting for the back.

Grandma Minnie is still cutting out biscuits and laughing, most likely at me.

"Ash! Order up!"

I load up a tray, carry it out to a four-top table and I am ridiculously careful to not even look in the vicinity of Mike and Eliza's table.

"Ash!" I hear Eliza hiss as I am turning to go back to the kitchen and I bite my lip, tucking the tray under my arm and turn.

Cooper has joined them, so I walk over and smile at him.

"Hi Cooper."

"Ashten," he grins, settling into the bench, putting his arm around Eliza.

This is good. At least I can avoid looking at the other side of the table.

"What can I get you?"

"What did you guys get?" Cooper asks Eliza and Mike. "I've only eaten here a couple of times."

I am careful to watch Eliza. I even have my back slightly turned to Mike so that I can just focus on Cooper.

"Don't order what Mike got, you can make that yourself. I got the French toast. It's amazing. They coat it in like crushed corn flakes or something."

Cooper makes a face. "Eh."

"Don't *eh*. It's amazing! And it's covered in strawberries and whipped cream! It's like the best of all worlds colliding."

"Eh."

I grin. I really like Eliza and Cooper together. He's good for her. He's just nuts enough himself to not let her have all the fun but he's a little more grounded than her overall.

If Katie and Luke are going to be the world's nicest couple and never fight, Eliza and Cooper are going to be the world's loudest couple. They both do everything at a volume that my mother always referred to as "outside voices".

"Hey, did you hear the news?" Cooper asks me, delaying his order and making me stay there forever.

I try my best to look relaxed and cheerful. "What's the news?"

"I'm moving to town!"

"Oh, I did hear that."

"Yep. So I can be a regular here too."

I smile. "When are you moving?"

"I start my new job in three weeks, so I'm moving in two. I'm going to crash with Mike until the wedding."

I finally look over at Mike and he's like the picture of a Saturday off. He's leaning back against the bench, one arm casually on the back of the bench, one hand holding the coffee he's sipping.

Apparently, I am the only one who is so tightly wound, I feel like I'm going to morph into Tigger here any minute.

I feel like Mike and Cooper would not live together well.

But I guess they have before, so maybe I'm wrong. And I think we've already established that I probably don't know the real Mike very well.

"That's great," I say. "So, what can I get you?"

"Do you guys have any sort of breakfast steak?"

"We have our breakfast chicken fried steak with biscuits and gravy."

"Perfect." He nods. "That's it. I'll have that. Extra gravy."

"Very healthy choice," Mike says, sipping his coffee.

"I'm on a diet. It's been rough."

"I'll have that right out, guys."

Mike smiles at me as I leave.

I swear.

What happened?

CHAPTER *Nineteen*

Sunday morning, I'm so distracted, I can barely remember to put on mascara.

This is not good.

Jesus, please help me to focus on what's important today.

Katie gets us to church, Eliza complains the whole way there and everything is super normal.

They both turn to look at me when Katie parks.

"Are you okay?"

I can't even keep track of how many times people have asked me this question lately.

"I'm fine," I say because that's what you say.

"No, you're not," Katie says.

"Yeah. What she said. Come on. The Time Nazi got us here ten minutes early so spill." Eliza is looking at me expectantly from the passenger seat.

This is so awkward. It's her brother we're talking about.

Eliza smirks. "This is about Mike, isn't it?"

"No."

"It is not good to lie. Especially in the church parking lot. That counts as a double lie."

Katie looks at Eliza. "Right. Show me a verse for that one."

"Hezekiah 2:17."

"You can't spout random old names and pretend they are books of the Bible."

Eliza grins. "Anyway."

I rub my forehead. This is so awkward. He's her brother.

"Look, there was obviously something between you two when we came in for breakfast yesterday," Eliza says. "The sparks were flying like crazy!"

I shake my head. "I don't think those were sparks."

"Dude, you need to take some classes in fire safety, because seriously."

Katie nods. "I mean, I could see sparks and I wasn't even there."

I shake my head.

Eliza keeps talking. "And I've never seen Mike this happy before. He was whistling yesterday. I think every dog in the neighborhood was at my back door because he whistled all day long."

Katie laughs.

If anything, Eliza's talk makes me more confused. I
take a deep breath and shrug it off. "It's nothing. I'm good.
I'm okay."

"Two lies in two minutes. Still on church property.
Girl, you'd better be praising God for grace today."

Katie laughs again and we climb out of the car.

It doesn't appear that Mike is at church yet and I make
sure that I park myself right in the middle of Katie and Eliza
in the row.

Eliza looks at me and shakes her head. "What, you
weren't comfortable last week?"

I sigh. Surely Daniel won't come back, but either way,
it's awkward enough without sitting right next to Mike and I
know he'll be here.

Mike walks in thirty seconds before music starts, so I
barely have time to smile politely at him before we have to
stand and start singing. And Luke, of course, saunters in
about two minutes before the last song ends.

I grip my Bible with both hands and Pastor Mark
comes to the stage, smiling at all of us.

I've never seen him not smiling.

What is it about pastors and smiling? Does it come
naturally? If you're of the grumpier disposition, are you not
called to be in ministry?

"Friends," he says. "Today is a good day."

Is it, Lord?

"Let's open our Bibles to Galatians, we are going to finish out the book today," he says.

He begins to read and I follow along, praying for concentration the entire time.

"'But may it never be that I would boast, except in the cross of our Lord Jesus Christ, through which the world has been crucified to me, and I to the world.'" Pastor Mark looks up at us. "I love this verse for two reasons and we're going to spend our whole morning on those two reasons," he smiles.

He wraps things up about forty minutes later. "In conclusion, what Paul is saying to our Galatian friends is that this world has no hold on us. We have died to it and we now have Christ and Christ alone. And that's where we can find our true selves, friends. It's not in the 'joys' of this world. It's not in friends, it's not in relationships, not in spouses or children or jobs or houses or cars. It's only in Christ."

He looks out over all of us and I know he makes eye contact with me. "I want to leave you with the final words of this book. 'The grace of our Lord Jesus Christ be with your spirit.'" He smiles at everyone. "Amen."

The worship team comes back up to play and we all stand and prepare to leave a few minutes later.

Luke stretches. "That was a great one. I'm really going to miss Galatians."

"I think he's doing Colossians next, so I'm sure it will be just as good," Katie says.

Eliza is looking at her watch. "Well. I need to go. Cooper is supposed to pick me up in three minutes so we can go check out caterers. Peace out, friends."

She leaves, waving to a few people as she walks out.

Mike looks over at me. "Good morning."

"Hi."

The tension is so thick you could probably vacuum it.

"Well, we need to go, too," Katie announces in a much louder voice than she needs.

"We do?"

"Sure, sure," she says, scooting around Luke into the aisle. "Remember? That thing?"

"What thing?"

"That thing I told you about? That thing we have to do today?"

"We don't have a thing."

"That thing. I told you about the thing."

"We don't do anything. I distinctly remember you saying that we didn't have anything today."

She is trying so hard and Luke is failing so badly.

I know that she's trying to get him out of there so it will just be Mike and me.

Katie is visibly annoyed and she finally takes Luke's hand and waves at us. "Bye, guys! See you later!"

"What thing?" Luke asks as they walk up the aisle.

If the tension was thick before, it's suffocating now.

My poor Bible has never been gripped this hard before.

"Well," I say.

"So," Mike says at the same time.

Then we both do that little pretend laugh when you accidentally talk over the other person and he waves his hand.

"You go first," he says.

"Oh, I was going to say, I guess I'd better be going."

"Oh, yeah. Sure, definitely."

"What were you going to say?"

"I was just, uh, going to see if you had plans today," he says, tucking his Bible under his arm and shoving his hands into his pockets. "It's a really nice morning. We could take a walk or something. Maybe get lunch. I don't know."

My Bible will never be the same. There might be a permanent print of my hand in it.

"Um, sure," I say, trying to sound all casual but instead, I sound like a chipmunk who has been inhaling helium. "That sounds great!"

"Okay. So do you want me to follow you home and then we can take my car?"

I suddenly remember that Katie drove me here and she has already left.

"Wait, I rode here with Katie," I say. I go down the aisle and out the front door and her car is long gone.

I have a feeling this was a planned abandonment.

So kind.

I look at Mike and he shrugs. "Well, now we don't have to drop off your car."

I guess that's true.

I follow Mike out the door and his silver truck is on the edge of the parking lot, like way, way back in the boonies.

By the time we get to the truck, I feel like we've already taken our walk. There are like three miles of open spaces between his truck and the door, so maybe Mike is one of those people who advocates taking the stairs instead of the elevator and all that stuff.

Heart disease prevention or something.

"Sorry," he says, unlocking his truck and holding open the passenger door for me. "I figure, I *can* walk, you know?"

I climb in and realize that he parks light years away to save the open spots and there's a little twinge deep in my chest.

He really is a nice person.

He slides into the driver's seat. "There's a really nice little path close to your house," he says. "I actually run it almost every morning."

I don't tell him I saw him there once, I nod. "Sure."

"And then maybe we could go get tacos or something at that little Mexican food place up the street?"

"Sure." I sound like a broken record.

He starts driving to my house and I am racking my brain for things to talk about, if for no other reason than to break the incredibly awkward silence.

I am feeling the awkwardness in my tendons.

"So," he says.

"So," I say at the same time.

More pretend laughing.

There is a huge part of me that wants him to take me home so I can crawl into my bed and die.

This never happened with Daniel. He always had something to say. I did a lot of listening. Which wasn't my favorite but at least I wasn't sitting here trying to think of anything possible to talk about.

"Go ahead," Mike says to me, turning toward our street.

"Oh, no, you can go."

"I insist."

I don't even actually remember what I was going to say now. "Do you feel like you've completely settled in here in Carrington Springs?"

He nods. "I do, actually. My apartment is nice."

"Didn't want to buy a house like Eliza?"

"Lyzie needs enough help with her house that I already feel like I own one," Mike says and I smile. I have seen Mike over there working often.

Even before he moved here, he would be over at her house, replacing her sprinkler system or whatever she needed.

He pulls to a stop in front of Eliza's house and we climb out.

"Are you going to change?" he asks.

"No, but I'll drop off my Bible real quick." I'm wearing jeans and a nicer T-shirt. I duck inside, drop my Bible on the couch, take a deep breath and go back out there.

He's waiting on the sidewalk.

"Ready?"

"I think so."

"Okay. I usually go this way, but I think there are a few ways to get there."

He starts off down the path the same way I've gone in the past. We keep up a pretty good pace, which is nice, because I'm so focused on keeping up that I don't feel the awkwardness of the silence that has once again fallen over us.

This is weird.

"Okay, Ashten," Mike says, holding out a hand to stop me when we are out of my little subdivision and smack in the middle of the path that leads through the wooded area around us.

I look up at him and then around us and it feels like we are the only people in the woods right now.

Well, at least no one else has to suffer through this.

"Look, I need to apologize," Mike says. "I know that we got off on the wrong foot and I've already apologized for that, but I want you to know that I've been informed that I said something really hurtful when I asked you out and I want you to know, I did not mean it that way at all."

Eliza.

Meddler.

I take a deep breath and start walking again, mostly because Mike's brown eyes are like boring into mine and I can only do that for so long before getting super antsy.

"Did Eliza tell you?" I ask.

"She asked me to protect the names of the guilty."

I smirk. "So much for secrets."

"Ashten, I'm so sorry. When I said 'despite everything', I in no way was referring to anything wrong with you. I really was talking about myself."

I look at him. "What do you mean?"

"I mean, I don't...I haven't really dated people. I mean, I've gone out a few times over the years, but never more than once or twice and never with someone I already kind of knew. I don't do this. After my parents...I mean, it was

314

just Lyzie and me. And I think I got it in my head that caring about someone meant getting hurt. But God's been showing me so much lately about confidence."

I immediately stop but he takes another two steps before realizing I'm no longer beside him. He turns and looks at me. "You okay?"

"What, specifically about confidence?" Surely we haven't both been learning the same thing.

"Just that I can let go. I don't have to be in control or freak out when something happens. And trust me, you have no idea how impossible it would have been for me to say that, even six months ago." He sighs. "There's a verse in Hebrews talking about how we can approach the throne of grace with confidence, because Jesus has already been tempted just as we have been. And I realized, Jesus most likely lost His earthly dad too. So He knew the pain of loss and when He died on the cross, He lost his Heavenly Father for a little while as well."

I am shaking my head from the minute he mentions the word "Hebrews".

What are the odds?

"What?" he asks.

"What?"

"Why are you shaking your head like that?"

"Want to know what verses God's really been pointing out to me constantly lately?"

"Sure."

"Hebrews 4."

He grins. "Funny how that happens. What have you been learning about it?"

I tell him a little bit, and as I'm talking, I'm realizing, little by little, things are relaxing between us.

It doesn't feel weird.

Or maybe it does and I have my hands shoved so deeply into my pockets, I can't feel the weirdness in my tendons anymore.

We keep walking, still talking and we get to the park a few minutes later. There are a bunch of people here today. Families, couples, kids. Lots and lots of dogs.

"Want to keep walking or head back?"

I shrug. "We can keep walking."

We make the loop around the park and head back to the path, back to my house.

"Ashten?"

I almost don't even hear him. I turn to look at him and he's not beside me anymore, so I turn around and he's stopped a foot or two back up the path.

Something about the look on his face makes my immediately feel like I'm wearing some sort of corset.

"Yeah?"

"Do you think that..." His voice trails off and he clears his throat. "Do you think that maybe, you might consider going out with me...sometime?"

He's really cute when he's nervous.

I smile, trying to force myself to breathe easier, pulling my hands out of my pockets and exhaling. "Aren't we getting tacos tonight?"

He laughs, but it's a nervous laugh and I bite back another smile.

Poor guy.

"I kind of meant more like a real date."

"Tacos aren't a real date?"

"Not really." He looking at me expectantly and I nod.

Funny how something I never would have considered even a month ago is now something that I'm actually excited about. "Okay."

His whole face lights up. "Really? Are you sure?"

I grin and start back walking. He catches up in less than a second, smiling over at me.

"What?" I ask him.

"Nothing. I just...I don't know. I have a good feeling about this."

Ribcage is instantly corseted again.

We keep walking and he gently, carefully, takes my hand, weaving his fingers through mine.

And when I look up at him, he's smiling down at me.

Erynn Mangum

318

EPILOGUE

They say that all good stories end with a wedding.

So I'm going to end mine with one.

I wipe away tears as the preacher closes his Bible and urges my two very dear friends to turn to the church full of friends and family. "It is my great honor to introduce to you, for the first time, Mr. and Mrs. Luke Brantley!"

The crowd bursts into applause. Luke grins so wide I'm worried about a sprain in his facial muscles, he dips his new bride down and kisses her again, to the cheers and whistles of the audience.

Katie is blushing and gorgeous and I've never seen my friend so happy. It's the kind of happy that makes you immediately filled with joyful tears.

So, Eliza and I exchange looks and cry.

The music starts and Luke and Katie run up the aisle, the cameras flashing as they leave the sanctuary, paparazzi shooting the end to my dear friend's very own Happily Ever After.

Eliza links arms with Luke's brother at the midway point on the stage like we were instructed to do and starts off behind Katie and Luke. I see her toss a flirtatious wink to Cooper who got himself possibly the best seat in the house.

He blows Eliza a kiss, the white gold on his two week old ring shining in the lights.

It's still so weird to see him with a ring. And to think they have already been married for two weeks.

I smile at Luke's old college roommate, we meet at the spot and follow Eliza down the aisle. I briefly scan the audience and I catch his eye right before we leave the sanctuary.

He's grinning and I don't think I've ever seen his eyes sparkle so much, except for maybe two weeks ago at Eliza's wedding.

The photographers usher the wedding party into a tiny room to the side of the sanctuary. There's the happy shouts of joy, the clicks of the cameras, the signing of the marriage license.

Katie is radiant.

"Okay, now as soon as the sanctuary has been cleared, we will go back in and take our pictures, so no one leave, got it?" The photographer tries to sound all lighthearted, but I know that she means business.

Katie is looking around. "Eliza, where's my little bag with the lipstick?"

Eliza looks at her. "What bag?"

"That little lavender bag? You didn't lose it, did you?"

"Um, no. But I have not seen a little lavender bag ever in my life. Much less today."

"Oh Eliza!"

I step in. "I got it, Katie. It's probably back in the room we were getting ready in. I'll go find it."

I hand Eliza my flowers. "Make sure you don't lose these."

"Oh for goodness sakes, you can't lose something you never saw!"

I grin at her and sneak through the door before the photographer can notice I'm leaving and have a fit.

I close the door quietly behind me, turn and almost run right into him.

"There's the most beautiful girl in the room."

I'm pretty sure I blush like twelve shades of red.

Mike grins at me. "Ash, I'm serious here, but I've gotten very used to seeing you in these kind of dresses every two weeks. Any chance we could keep this up? Who else do you know who needs a bridesmaid? It could be a new hobby."

"Yeah, that would be like the most expensive hobby on the planet," I say.

He reaches for my hand and I squeeze his and then start down the empty hallway. "Wait, where are you going?"

"Katie forgot her lipstick!"

"Oh my gosh, can the wedding even go on?"

I send him a look over my shoulder, my dress swishing back behind me and he grins.

"What?"

"Do you not remember how panicked we all were about the Something Blue at Eliza's that went missing?"

He catches up with me and shakes his head as we basically run down the hall. "It's the curse of every bride to panic at least once over something ridiculous, I think. You'll probably do it, too."

"Eh. We'll see."

"Yes. We will." He grins at me as we get to the room and I narrow my eyes at him. "What?"

"Why are you smiling like that?"

He is still grinning. "Your day is coming, Wadeley. Just you wait."

"It sounds ominous."

He leans down and kisses me.

I blink at him.

"I'm just saying. Our day is coming." He smiles at me again, but this time, it's so sweet. He gently rubs my cheek, winks and then turns to the room. "What are we looking for again? Hairspray?"

I half shake my head to clear the brain. "No, it's a bag." I see it over by Katie's overnight bag and I pick it up and wave as I run back down the hall. "Thanks!"

I get back in the room and my hair is nearly singed by the glare from the photographer, but I hold up the lavender bag all *see? I had to!* to her and she sighs.

322

Katie, though, is ecstatic. "You found it!" she squeals and grabs it from me. "Thank you!"

Eliza is looking at me. "What happened to you?"

"What?"

"You're all flushed and weird looking."

I roll my eyes, trying to poke back a wayward curl into a loose bobby pin. "Well, thanks. I was running down the hall."

"No," Eliza says, shaking her head. "No, that's not it." She grins. "You saw Mike."

I sigh.

"Ah ha! I knew it." She grins and then hands me both bouquets of flowers and reaches to help me fix the bobby pin. "You'll be a beautiful bride, soon to be sister."

At the rate my cheeks are heating up lately, I won't need to apply blush for years.

Katie puts on her lipstick and then looks at Eliza and me as Eliza takes her flowers back, done with my hair.

"Well," she says, grinning at us.

"You're married," I say and I can feel the tears pricking again.

"You look gorgeous," Eliza says.

"So do you guys."

"All right, wedding party! I need everyone to convene in the sanctuary!" the photographer yells.

Katie reaches for my right hand and for Eliza's left and the look on her face is not helping me hold the tears in.

"I waited for years for this," Katie whispers as everyone starts to leave the room.

Eliza grins at her. "Worth the wait?"

Katie sniffs. "No. Not just this. *This.*" She squeezes our hands and I can see tears in her eyes. "I can't believe that God blessed me with not only a husband but also two sisters."

"Good grief, woman. My mascara was perfect," Eliza is sucking air in through the nose and out through the mouth, waving her hand in front of her face.

I laugh and loop an arm around both of their necks and hug my friends – my sisters – close.

"We need the bride!" the photographer is less than pleased that we are late and Katie waves a hand by her face, nodding.

"Coming! We're coming."

I follow the girls out and into the sanctuary, lining up where I'm told to stand.

This life is so crazy and tiring and messy and joyful. And two years ago, I sat in a bowling alley by myself and cried because, even though I have family and cousins and aunts and uncles to spare, I was still alone.

I sneak a look to the right and the tears are quick. Eliza, Katie, Luke. I can see Cooper and Mike waiting off to the side, laughing about something together by the pews.

I'm reminded of the verse from Psalm 68 Katie wrote on a card in my bridesmaid's gift.

God sets the lonely in families.

I look around me and my smile doesn't need to be forced for the cameras.

Yes, He does indeed.

THE *End*